PRAISE FOR
The Detective's Assistant

A *BOOKLIST* EDITORS' CHOICE

★ "**Excitement and intrigue** without an intense sense of fear or danger—a remarkable balance that keeps this novel **accessible and captivating**....With **skilled writing** that conveys the excitement of detective work, the appeal of history, and Nell's authentic, good-humored personal growth, **this is one for the ages**."
—*THE BULLETIN*, STARRED REVIEW

★ "**Chicanery, American history, and lots of excitement.** An author's note explains that Kate Warne was a real person who did many of the things described in the book, making this **a great title for promoting women's history**. But even if Kate were purely fictional, Nell—strong-willed yet scared, tough but needy— makes **a solid heroine**." —*BOOKLIST*, STARRED REVIEW

"**Hannigan's quick pace and Nell's spunky voice** successfully suspend readers' disbelief, and the author manages to pack **an amazing amount of historical tidbits** in along the way. A **rousing** fictional account of the remarkable career of **a pioneering woman**."
—*KIRKUS REVIEWS*

"Hannigan makes skillful use of period details, bringing the novel's threads together in **a nail-biting conclusion**. Nell is **a fearless, no-nonsense heroine**, and her dry-witted narration drives this **rollicking historical escapade**." —*PUBLISHERS WEEKLY*

"**Nell is an irrepressible character: spirited, thoughtful, and intuitive**....Although there are plenty of **madcap adventures**, grief and the longing for a home are at the forefront of the story.... Recommend to readers who enjoy **adventure, history, and stories featuring independent, strong-minded girls**."
—*SCHOOL LIBRARY JOURNAL*

The Detective's Assistant

By Kate Hannigan

LITTLE, BROWN AND COMPANY
NEW YORK BOSTON

For Norm

Copyright © 2015 by Kate Hannigan
Interior art copyright © 2015 John Hendrix

Little, Brown and Company

Hachette Book Group
1290 Avenue of the Americas, New York, NY 10104
Visit us at lb-kids.com

Little, Brown and Company is a division of Hachette Book Group, Inc.
The Little, Brown name and logo are trademarks of Hachette Book Group, Inc.

The publisher is not responsible for websites (or their content) that are not owned by the publisher.

First Paperback Edition: April 2016
First published in hardcover in April 2015 by Little, Brown and Company

The Library of Congress has cataloged the hardcover edition as follows:

Hannigan, Kate.
    The detective's assistant / by Kate Hannigan. — First edition.
        pages cm.
    Summary: "In 1859, eleven-year-old Nell goes to live with her aunt, Kate Warne, the first female detective for Pinkerton's National Detective Agency. Nell helps her aunt solve cases, including a mystery surrounding Abraham Lincoln, and the mystery of what happened to Nell's own father. Includes author's note and bibliographic references"— Provided by publisher.
    ISBN 978-0-316-40351-1 (hardcover) — ISBN 978-0-316-40350-4 (ebook) — ISBN 978-0-316-40352-8 (library edition ebook)   [1. Mystery and detective stories.   2. Pinkerton's National Detective Agency—Fiction.   3. Aunts—Fiction.   4. Orphans—Fiction.   5. Sex role—Fiction.   6. Lincoln, Abraham, 1809–1865—Fiction.   7. Chicago (Ill.)—History— 19th century—Fiction.]   I. Title.
    PZ7.H198158Det 2015
    [Fic]—dc23

                                                                                    2014015131

Paperback ISBN 978-0-316-40349-8

10 9 8 7 6 5 4 3

RRD-C

Printed in the United States of America

"WE NEVER SLEEP"

Chapter 1

In Which I Find Myself on the Doorstep of a Pickled Onion

You're expecting me to do what?" snapped a peevish voice from the other side of the heavy wooden door. It opened just a few inches to allow a single blue eye to survey me up and down. "Take in this gangly urchin you claim is one of my kin? One look tells me the child hasn't made the acquaintance of a bar of lye in a good many years, not to mention been in the same two-mile vicinity of a comb."

I quickly ran my hands over my head to smooth down my hair from the center, lest she start commenting on the size of my ears.

"Why, yes, Mrs. Warne," said the Right Reverend, sliding his pointy black boot forward just a hint to keep her door from slamming shut on his petition. "You are the waif's last relation in the world. Without you, the child is destined to a most piteous life in the orphan asylum."

"Surely someone will come and take the, the…"

"Girl," the Right Reverend declared, giving his throat a good clearing.

Could she not tell that for herself?

I studied her eye through the crack in the door just to see if the woman was wearing spectacles. Surely her vision was failing, because I was obviously not some stinky schoolboy standing here before her. My clothes might have looked a bit on the masculine side, what with having to take my brother's best traveling coat for the long journey to Chicago. And the brown trousers might not be something you see every day on a fancy city girl. But what chores could a body get done on a farm while wearing a dress, I'd like to know?

My aunt stared back at me through the inch or so of open door, inspecting me like I was a sack of mealy flour. Then she added, without the least bit of conviction, "She'll make someone a lovely daughter someday."

I decided to win her over with my charm, so I smiled up at her with a powerful grin that showed all my teeth. I squeezed one cheek with my finger and forced a dimple. She was the last living relative I had in this world, and I was not going to let her turn me away.

My aunt recoiled like I'd just presented her with a toad, pinching her lips so tight, they made a straight line across the lower part of her face—or what I could see of her face.

I gave it another try. I licked both my hands and ran them through my shortish hair, slicking down any clumps that were sticking up. Then I batted my long eyelashes at her like a graceful doe. I was going for irresistible, but I might have fallen short.

"What's the matter with her eyes?"

The Right Reverend draped his arm around my shoulder, pretending to appear fatherly. But his skinny fingers pinched my shoulder something awful. I got the hint and quickly stopped my eye-batting. I returned to hair-slicking.

He let out a sigh that was about as deep and long as the whistle on our locomotive. I could tell that the Right Reverend wasn't about to head back to the middle of New York State with me in tow. After our long ride down from Chemung County, him and me had spent enough quality time together to last a lifetime. Besides, that man could smell a sucker from fifty paces away, and he wasn't going to give up easily. He had followed the trail to my aunt's door like a coonhound on the hunt.

"Between you and me and the gaslights, Mrs. Warne," he said, dabbing at a faint layer of nervous sweat that had formed above his lip, "the older mites at the orphanage do not have the same appeal as the babies. I don't share this dreadful perspective, mind you. But as a girl of ten summers, dear Cornelia here doesn't stand a chance of ever getting adopted."

"Eleven," I announced, though nobody had seen fit to ask me. "Or thereabouts."

And then, acting like I'd just spontaneously caught fire, the Right Reverend snatched his hand off my shoulder, pressed some papers in my aunt's direction, and took off down the boardinghouse stairs. She called for him to stop, but he did not. I stared down the hallway after him, wondering if I should feel a pang of worry. But I couldn't muster even a faint hiccup of remorse to see the backside of that man.

My aunt's entire head was outside the door now, but her body still blocked me from coming into her room. Her face was average-looking, though it could have been pretty if it weren't lined with so much crankiness. I had always envied cornflower-blue eyes like hers, and the lashes framing them were long and brown like feathers on a whip-poor-will. So pinched and prim like she was, I could tell she was on a fast road to becoming a dowdy old matron. I hadn't seen enough of her teeth to be sure, but I figured her age to already be about twenty-five.

I picked up the yellowish papers off the floor and held them out for her to take. She just stared at me and made no motion to invite me inside.

"How did you find me?" she asked.

Her expression was sour with a hint of bitterness, and I was immediately reminded of a pickled onion. Her mouth was pinched so tight again, I half expected her jaw to squeak when she moved it.

"Right Reverend found you, ma'am. Not me."

"I haven't spoken to anyone in your family since . . ."

"The accident," I said, helping fill the gap. "And Warnes are your family, too, by the way."

She scoffed and gave me a hard look. I could tell she was sizing me up. So I gave her a hard look right back.

"Accident?" she laughed, though the sound that came out of her was anything but joyful. "Is that what they're calling it?"

"There's no 'they' calling it anything," I corrected, a little peevishness coloring the edges of my voice now, too. "There's just me. Ain't no Warnes left in Chemung County except me. I'm the very last one."

"Your mother?"

"Whooping cough."

"Uncle Silas?"

"Drowned."

"Aunt Martha?"

"Scalded."

"Your brothers?"

"One of scarlet fever."

"The other?"

"Fell off the roof last December. Died the next week."

She made a little *hmmph* noise, as if that satisfied her. But her eyes didn't go soft or anything like she understood the heavy sack of sorrows I was carrying around. She just kept staring at me until I finally had to look away. My eyes were beginning to sting.

I blinked real fast, but not so I'd look irresistible this time. It was because I missed everybody so much. If any one of them was still back at the farm, filling his or her lungs with deep breaths of fresh air, then I wouldn't have to be standing here right now. But with each passing, my world got smaller and smaller, until they were all gone. And here I was in Chicago.

Alone.

My eyes were wet as I picked at my fingernails.

"And your father was the very last to go," my aunt said with a little *tsk-tsk* sound. "Cornelius always did look after Cornelius. Tell me—how did he meet his Maker? Hanged from a lawman's noose, I assume?"

"Shot. But he wasn't doing no wrong. He was helping people," I said. Then added softly, "Some bad men shot him dead. It was a crime."

She went silent, and I was thankful she didn't make hay about my daddy getting himself killed. I didn't know all the particulars of how it happened, but my heart told me he was pure and true.

"It was not your daddy's fault, you say?" Her voice came so low, I had to lean forward against the dark doorframe a bit so I'd catch it. "Just like the day he killed my Matthew, his own brother? In what you call an *accident*."

"Exactly," I said, trying to match my voice to hers, low and serious. She was a pickled onion, and I wasn't about to let her intimidate me. "If you'd let me explain it, you'd understand. My daddy wouldn't never hurt a fly. He didn't mean to kill your Matthew, Aunt Kitty."

"Don't call me that," she snapped, stepping aside and finally allowing me to leave the dismal hallway and enter her room. Her dark blue skirts rustled as she walked, and her movements were quick. I noticed she was more slender than I thought she'd be, and taller, too.

I looked all around the room. It wasn't the worst boardinghouse I'd seen in Chicago, but then again I'd

8

been in town only one day. A boiled-cabbage smell hung in the air downstairs in the parlor, but up here on the third floor it wasn't so bad. Just stuffy and hot. The sound of a horse's shrill whinny on the street below drifted in through an open window, but no breeze.

"I'm not in Chemung County anymore, Cornelia. Here in Chicago, I go by Kate."

"Well, don't go calling me Cornelia," I countered, pushing a lock of my stringy hair away from my eyes and tromping across the room. My boots were a few sizes too big, and they made a satisfying *clip-clomp* sound on her wooden floor. I let my carpetbag drop beside me and reached up to touch the angled wall above my head. This room must have been an attic once. "All my friends back in New York call me Cornie."

The Pickled Onion laughed. Only it sounded joyful this time and not, as I expected, meant to hurt my feelings. Her laugh was the bouncy kind that starts somewhere in the pit of the stomach and leaps up the body like a jackrabbit, finally coming to rest around the eyes.

"What arrogance," she finally said. "How could

Cornelius saddle you with such a dreadful name? Especially when you're already marked with his looks—you are the spitting image of that man. But *Cornelia*? Sounds like a fungus that plagues a vegetable garden."

I opened my mouth to protest, but I had not one word at my disposal. For a girl who'd spent her whole life perfecting the art of arguing—with my brothers, my mother, my mule, and until just a few months ago with my daddy—suddenly I was caught short.

And the reason why was simple. It was because every single, solitary day that I'd been walking this good green earth, I'd been complaining about the name Cornelia.

"And Cornie?" she continued. "That's no better. Are you sure those were friends who called you that?"

I scrunched up my eyes and gave my aunt a look. She was starting to put me in a mood. I couldn't tell if she was poking fun at me or flat-out handing me an insult.

Either way, I'd just about had enough of her.

"I shall call you Nell," she said, stepping over to a straight-backed chair and perching there. She folded her hands neatly in her lap as if she were Queen Victoria herself on the throne. "It sounds much less ridiculous than either of the other options."

My own hands, which seconds ago were balled up and ready to start swinging, dropped to my sides like a couple of overripe apples from a tree. And my jaw did the same thing, hanging open wide enough to catch a dragonfly.

Because Nell Warne was just about the prettiest name I'd ever heard. And suddenly it was all mine.

Chapter 2

❦

In Which I Share My Woe with My Best Friend, Jemma

August 3, 1859

Dear Jemma,

By the time you read this, I will be gone from these parts. As I write, I have packed my bag and am sitting in the tree out front of Right Reverend Abernathy's door. You might recall him, or if you're smart, you might not want to. He is the preacher who runs the Chemung County Home for Orphans and Pathetic Souls.

I believe that's the name of this place, though I might not have it exactly right. It's where I wound up living these past months.

I am sorry to break the news to you, but my dear daddy, Cornelius Jeremiah Warne, has died. This might come as a shock to your mama and papa, since your family was friends with us Warnes for so long. That is, before you had to move so far away from us. Your papa, so thick and strong like a maple tree, he never made a fuss about helping my daddy split logs or round up cattle when they strayed. I recall our fathers were good friends because of it. But now my daddy, Cornelius J. Warne, is splitting logs with the angels.

I hope my letter does not cause anyone to shed tears. I believe I have done enough of that for the whole town, what with Daddy's dying coming so soon after my brother Zeke's funeral last Christmas. And the others, but I've told you about them already.

There is no sound like the one an empty house makes. You know the lonesome call of the whip-poor-will, I am sure. And I imagine that plenty of times you have sat and listened to the wind rustle leaves at night. But nothing reminds a body of how alone they are in the world than footsteps in an empty house. At first I didn't mind when the Right Reverend showed up and took me to the Home for Orphans down here in town. I was just happy not to be haunting that old house like a teary-eyed ghost.

But I will not be staying in this orphan asylum another day, and for that I am eternally grateful. Did I already mention there was not even a bed for me to sleep on with all these hungry children packed in here? That might take a whole ~~seperat editional~~ nother letter to describe. Let me just say the Right Reverend found me

a long-lost Warne kin who lives in Chicago.
I do not recall her well, since she left
some years back.

But family is family, and I'll stick with
her like a tick on a fat dog.

Very truly your friend,
Cornie

Chapter 3

In Which My Aunt Wants Nothing to Do with Me

I awoke in the morning with a crick in my neck. That's what sleeping curled up like a cat in a lumpy parlor chair will do for a body. The wooden armrests had seemed a comfortable place to lay my head last night. But as I got to my feet, I was as stiff as a hitching post. And sleeping in my dusty clothes hadn't helped much either. But Aunt Kitty said it would be best—she wanted to get an early start this morning, and that would save us time.

It's not that I expected Aunt Kitty to give up her bed in the back room last night. So I can't quite blame her for the lack of hospitality she supplied. And maybe the kitchen was closed in the evening when she gathered up food for my supper. That meager bowl of cabbage broth—so bare, I wouldn't even call it a soup—failed to satisfy my hearty appetite. I planned to make up for it at breakfast today, and I could already smell the heavenly aroma of coffee summoning me downstairs to the table.

"Let's get a move on, Aunt Kitty," I said, tapping on her door. Her sleeping quarters in the second room weren't much bigger than a closet, but I already knew where I'd fit my bed. I had peeked in yesterday, when she was off scrounging up my sad supper. And I figured I could tuck a mattress and pretty iron bed frame right next to the tall wardrobe. Then we could stay up nights talking and reading together like chums.

I knocked again, a little stronger this time. "There's probably a mountain of boiled eggs in the dining room with our names on them. And biscuits with jam, too."

I expected Aunt Kitty to still be snuggled under her covers tight like a caterpillar in a cocoon, but she was not. She suddenly pulled open her door and swept

17

right out of the bedroom, her hair perfectly arranged and her dark blue skirts swishing as she passed.

"I am ready to go, Nell, but not to breakfast," she announced, giving one of the gloves on her hand a firm tug. "We will proceed over to Wabash Avenue, where there has recently been built the Home for the Friendless. I believe it might make a more appropriate environment for you than what I can provide. I will leave you there. It is that simple."

Simple? It was that simple for her to give me over to strangers?

Her words made me stagger backward a few steps. I knew better than to believe the sound of that place— *Home for the Friendless*. It might seem like a shelter from the storm, but it really was another asylum packed with a bunch of mangy orphans ready to filch my last possessions while I slept. There was no way I was letting my aunt abandon me there.

"Your place is plenty big—" I began. But she didn't want to hear a thing from me. She just pointed at my carpetbag on the floor near the door and marched off. So I grabbed the handle and followed after her down the staircase, squeezing past a few boarders heading up from the breakfast table and trailing a mouthwatering smell of bacon.

We reached the street and headed east toward Lake Michigan, where the sun had just climbed out from under its thick, purplish-pink covers. I hoped the folks over at the Home for the Friendless might still be under their covers, too. If they were, maybe they wouldn't hear our knocking. Or maybe my aunt had no plans to knock—maybe she was just going to sit me down on the front stoop to wait until some sorry caretaker opened the door and found me there.

"Aunt Kitty," I protested, clomping my brown boots behind her through the dusty August morning. "I'm trying to tell you that your place at the boarding-house is fine enough for me. I don't take up too much space—"

"It is not about space, Nell. It is about what's right. And I do not think it's appropriate for a young girl like you to live in a boardinghouse."

"Then why don't you and me just move? Get a farm somewhere, or a house?"

She stopped her fast walking and turned to face me, her eyes flashing. I had to draw up short to keep from smacking right into her.

"Buy a house? With what money? I can't imagine Cornelius left you a vast inheritance. More like a few poker debts to settle. And I have my own life to lead. It cannot involve caring for a helpless girl."

I couldn't tell if she'd said *helpless* or *hopeless*. I told her I could find myself a job, earn a few coins to cover the cost of things. But she only let out a bitter chuckle and told me I was *naive*.

I didn't know what that word meant, but I suspected it was no compliment.

"Besides, you and me are all the family that's left, Aunt Kitty," I said, hitching my wool trousers up a bit. "We've got to stick together."

"We have to do no such thing, Nell. We hardly know each other. Am I supposed to alter my entire life in order to accommodate you? I think not. I apologize if the truth hurts, but let's face it: family is something you make; it is the people you choose to be with. Not the ones you're stuck with."

She might as well have elbowed me in the stomach,

the way her words took my breath away. I watched her walk on down the street and turn south on what must have been Wabash Avenue, and so I made my feet follow along behind. But it was like I was moving through a haze, my senses having turned numb.

We went on that way, with her crisp footsteps tip-tapping down the wooden sidewalk and my boots shuffling along after her, until we reached another intersection. There was a great commotion up ahead that was causing people to gather in clumps and crane their necks for a glimpse. I heard a few shouts and hollers from the street, even the shrill protesting from a horse, but couldn't see what was happening.

I set my bag down and scrambled up a small hawthorn tree so as to get a better view of the scene. And I saw right away what was going on. Two colossal brutes were fighting in front of a stone building just ahead of us, blocking the route in either direction. And the crowd was growing thicker as the wrestling match heated up. I saw Aunt Kitty try to squeeze by on the right, but there was no getting through. Then she stepped to her left but was pinched in from that direction as well.

What I noticed next came as a jolt, and I had to rub my eyes to make sure I wasn't seeing things. A long-armed street thug was reaching his hands into every coat, bag, and pocket he could find as the folks in the crowd, distracted as they were by the two sparring hooligans, stood there unaware. He had his own bag, a deep thing of stained black fabric, into which he was tossing all his ill-gotten loot. And if I didn't act fast, this sly picker of pockets would be helping himself to my aunt's money at any second.

"Aunt Kitty!" I hollered, swinging out of the tree like a crazed squirrel and racing to her side. She turned just in time to see the tattered sleeve of the thief emerge from her bag, dirty hand clutching her coin purse. And as Aunt Kitty grabbed for his arm, the scoundrel pushed her down and tried to run off.

"Give that back," I snarled. And with one swift stomp of my foot, I crashed the heel of my big brown boot onto his toes. "Pickpocket afoot! Pickpocket afoot!"

The bandit let out a howl and began hopping on one leg, which allowed me to snatch Aunt Kitty's coin purse right from his hand. I quickly helped my aunt to her feet, and we pushed our way back from the crowd. Our timing couldn't have been better, because in those few moments when all eyes turned from the brawny brawlers to our yelping thief, the crowd suddenly realized they'd been had. Hands frantically slipped into pockets and bags and coats, only to discover wallets gone. And they pounced on the skinny pickpocket like a pack of wolves.

"Nell, how did you know what he was doing?" gasped Aunt Kitty as she leaned heavily on my arm. "Though I've injured my knee, you have spared me a great loss. All my savings were in that purse."

I shrugged my shoulders and stared down at my feet, my heel still tingling from the stomping I'd given that thief. My old boots had sure come in handy when I needed them.

Aunt Kitty gazed down on them, too, then lifted her eyes to meet mine. She studied my face for a moment or two, which made me feel a good deal uncomfortable for the fuss, and then she finally spoke.

"That was very brave, Nell. And I thank you."

I wasn't expecting a kind word from her, and suddenly my cheeks felt hot with embarrassment. So I quickly retrieved my bag and looked over to see what was happening to the pickpocket. He was sprawled pathetically on the wooden sidewalk now, propping himself up on one elbow and seeming to reflect on the scene before him. The brawling brutes had run off. And his black bag was ripped open and empty, the contents probably recovered by their owners.

As the crowd wandered off, the stone building ahead of us came into view. I saw a few scrawny boys leaning out the open upstairs windows, hooting and whistling at the fallen pickpocket on the street below. Some more of them—these appeared younger and somehow dirtier—were jeering from behind a black iron fence that surrounded the yard. A few appeared skinny enough to slip through the bars. I read the wooden sign beside the front door and felt my heart clench in my chest:

CHICAGO HOME FOR THE FRIENDLESS

ESTABLISHED 1858

I couldn't move my gaze from the carved lettering. And I knew that Aunt Kitty, who was leaning on my shoulder beside me, was reading it, too.

I'd already done my time in one of these places, just

after my daddy died. The Right Reverend had told me I should be grateful to live there, a girl with no relations left in the world. But that orphans' home inspired no inklings of thankfulness in my heart. In fact, I could say with stone-cold certainty that I was never going back to such a place. Too many children crammed into rooms, never enough food to go around. And at night cries of such sadness, I had to plug my fingers in my ears to keep from joining in.

The heavy front door pushed open, and I watched a girl as pale as milk step outside, blinking in the sunlight. She let out a hacking cough and pulled her thin coat tighter around her shoulders, despite the August heat. When she turned to me, I recognized the wretchedness on her face. I knew it so well, it made me shudder. She spat on the sidewalk between us, then stared back at me with hopeless eyes. She was a candle that had been snuffed out.

I felt the urge to run for the train station and climb onto the next locomotive headed for Chemung County. But I could not go back there, with nobody but a few chickens to keep me company. The echoing emptiness of that old house left a gloom on me, like a layer of dust.

If I went back, I knew my bones would turn dry and crumble away.

But what else was I to do? The hollers of those skinny orphans at the fence, with their hateful, mocking laughter, pounded in my ears. If Aunt Kitty left me here, pressed in with hundreds of other unwanted souls, I could no longer complain of being alone. But I would be every bit as lonesome.

And each day my candle would burn down a little more, until it was nothing.

"Come along, Nell," Aunt Kitty finally said, gingerly turning herself around on her sore knee. "I will need your help getting back to the boardinghouse. And as for this Home for the Friendless, well, I believe we've had enough excitement for one day."

Chapter 4

In Which the Rent Is Inflated, and So Is My Sorry New Dress

I kept my chatting to a minimum for the rest of that day, lest I drove my aunt crazy with conversation until she marched me back to the orphan asylum. I think I tidied up our two rooms, not to mention changed and rechanged the pillow beneath her swollen knee at least six times before she finally suggested I go to sleep for the night. Even this morning, after rising again from my parlor chair, I decided not to join Aunt Kitty as she hobbled downstairs to breakfast. I was afraid my sizable appetite might scare her off.

"If your niece is to stay with you, Mrs. Warne,

I will have to raise your rent to fifteen dollars," came a high-pitched voice from the other side of the door. I opened it only to discover the enormous landlady, Mrs. Leticia Wigginbottom, filling the doorway. Dabbing at the sweat on her forehead with a lace hankie, she pushed into the room and collapsed dramatically into a rocking chair near the empty fireplace. She continued to talk as if my aunt were standing in the middle of the room, not me.

"I know you say the girl won't be staying but a few days. But should you decide to leave with her and find other accommodations, it would be a tragic loss, Mrs. Warne. You're one of my best tenants—nothing coarse about you, so tidy. You give the place a bit of class."

It seemed to tax all of Mrs. Wigginbottom's strength to make an appearance up here on the third floor of her boardinghouse. I suspected she sent one of her two servant girls to change the linens in the various rooms, which I discovered last night housed two other boarders (one who was fond of door slamming, another with a tendency for humming) and modern amenities (my aunt's way of delicately explaining the indoor toilet).

Mrs. Wigginbottom's cheeks were pink as she sat fanning herself with her hankie.

I was aghast at what she'd said. A rent of fifteen dollars was a dear price to pay—maybe too dear! Aunt Kitty was still downstairs, but she would surely rid herself of me the moment she learned this.

I'd have to earn my keep, and fast.

"I can sew and do a little knitting," I said frantically, wanting desperately to win over Mrs. Wigginbottom but feeling a little afraid to approach her, in case the chair she was sitting on should splinter beneath her impressive weight. "Give me what you need done around here, and take it off the rent."

Mrs. Wigginbottom tucked her hankie into the sleeve of her brown dress and gave me a curious look up and down.

"Mrs. Warne already does a bit of the laundry and sewing here, and it doesn't pay enough for two souls. Are you strong, young lady? Dressed in those boyish trousers, you do not appear to be a delicate flower."

I told her all the chores I used to do on the farm in Chemung County. Milking the cows and tending the chickens was how I greeted every morning. But did she have any cows for me in her backyard here in Chicago?

"A farm? Did your aunt work on the farm as well, Nell? And where is her husband, Mr. Warne? Did she leave him behind in the corncrib?"

"No, not at all, Mrs. Wigginbottom. Aunt Kitty left the day her Matthew got shot by my daddy. They were brothers, you see."

Mrs. Wigginbottom nodded like she understood, but her eyes told me otherwise. She asked if my daddy was in jail.

"He's in heaven now," I said, feeling my eyes start to well up at the thought of him. "Daddy saw the jailhouse for drinking and cheating at poker. But he never did time for shooting his brother. That was an accident, ma'am."

Mrs. Wigginbottom was on the edge of her seat now, which both made me proud as a storyteller that she was hanging on my every word, and caused me great concern for the fate of the rocking chair's legs. She asked me how my daddy made it to the pearly gates of heaven.

"Through prayer, ma'am. Mine mostly, since he wasn't the praying kind ..."

"No, child," she corrected. "I mean, how did your daddy die?"

I told her what I knew, which wasn't much. That he was shot just a few months back. That he was killed in the same woods where his brother Matthew had died a few years before. That there was something to do with slaves escaping to Canada. And that—unlike his brother's death—my daddy's passing was no accident.

"I am still piecing this patchwork quilt together, Mrs. Wigginbottom," I explained. "Most grown folks do not believe a person my age can handle the facts. So nobody bothers to tell me anything—except that I'm a hopeless orphan.

"I have an old friend in Canada who writes me letters. I believe she might know a thing or two—about how my daddy passed away and about how Aunt Kitty's husband died, too."

Suddenly Aunt Kitty appeared in the doorway. One look at her fierce blue eyes made it clear she'd overheard our conversation.

"My Matthew died when your daddy shot him, Nell. End of story. And if you want to pry into my private business, Mrs. Wigginbottom, you should interrogate me and not this silly girl."

I stood as still as a vase of peonies, fearing that the two of them were about to exchange words that would send me right back to the doorstep of the Home for the Friendless. My heart jumped up in my throat as I watched Mrs. Wigginbottom heave herself to her feet and straighten her cuffs, clearly insulted by the tone my aunt had taken.

"Your niece and I were just discussing the rent, Mrs. Warne, and how you plan to pay for it."

"That's right," I interrupted, deciding I'd better take Destiny into my own hands. I hastily searched for a way to cover the cost of keeping me here. And studying our landlady's heavy jowls and sausage-like fingers, I suddenly saw how I could help.

"With all the folks Mrs. Wigginbottom has to feed here, I was hoping to take over her marketing duties. I can do all her shopping each day—to the butcher, to the general store, to the vegetable market. This will save her having to carry those heavy groceries by herself. Won't that be a help?"

Mrs. Wigginbottom pulled at her tight, sweat-soaked collar and gave me a look of such relief, I knew I'd hit on the right thing.

"She looks as witless as a chicken," the landlady said, "but your niece is as clever as a fox, Mrs. Warne. You can start today, Nell. But not too early when prices are high. Wait until noontime to visit Lake Street, and look for the graying meats. That miserly butcher is willing to make a deal when the mutton starts to turn—but mind he doesn't put his thumb on the scale when he weighs it!"

It was many hours later when my work on Lake Street was finished. I'd bargained with Mr. Zenger, the German butcher, and come home with gray mutton. I'd done my best with Mr. O'Malley and his vegetables, but all I could scavenge from his wooden bins were a few wilted eggplants. And my arms and legs were still aching from the heavy sugarloaf I carried all the way from Mr. Lloyd's general store.

"Did you help Mrs. Wigginbottom put all the groceries away, Nell?" Aunt Kitty asked the moment I sat down and propped up my feet on the little wooden table by the window. The afternoon heat was stifling upstairs, and the lamb's wool I was using to stuff my oversize boots made my feet sweat. Even I could barely stand the smell. I peeked at Aunt Kitty to see if she was preparing to holler at me, but I saw her slip licorice from a silver tin and pop it into her mouth. She didn't bother offering me any.

"Of course I did," I snapped, not meaning to adopt my aunt's peckish ways. But hot is hot, and the layers of my brother's clothes were wet with sweat and itching me like fleas. "When I finished with her, I even put out a dish of milk for that sweet orange kitten that hangs around the back door. My work for the day is done."

"Not quite," she said, wrapping a cloth around her tender knee. "I want you to accompany me downtown. I have an appointment to keep, but afterward we can visit a few schools and asylums to see if they have room for you. Now wash up, and we'll go."

I started to point out that her knee was still mending and that she'd need me for at least another week. But Aunt Kitty put her hand up to shush me. And hot as I was, I decided that arguing with her would be about as useful as squabbling with the striped wallpaper. It wasn't going to get me anywhere. Instead, I would have to prove to her that I was useful to have around. So I headed into the tiny back room and began scrubbing my face and arms at the water basin.

"Hair," Aunt Kitty reminded.

"Why? I'm going to wear my old bonnet anyway."

She gave me another one of her looks. This one meant that I should stop talking and start combing.

"And it's time you put on a dress and let the world know you are of the female persuasion," she added. "So take off those boys' shirts and pants and pass them out to me. We'll give them to Mrs. Wigginbottom's girls for washing." Then she added at a whisper as she pulled the door shut, "Or burning."

"I heard that," I said. Then I caught a whiff of one of my undershirts, damp and stained yellow from sweat, and I began to cough.

Once I'd surrendered all the unsavory old clothes

to Aunt Kitty, I turned to a neat pile of fresh garments stacked on her bed. They were as white as eggshells and looked just as delicate. I picked up a petticoat, breathing in the fresh smell of lilac.

"It's so hot today, Aunt Kitty," I called through the closed door. "Do I have to put all these layers on?"

"Of course," came her reply. "It's not decent otherwise."

It felt a tinge awkward handling all these frills, but I'd laundered enough of my mama's linens to know what was what. I got started on the first layers, tugging the stifling black stockings up above my knees and then climbing into the long white drawers. Next I pulled on a cotton chemise with pretty white ribbons, thankful for its lack of sleeves. I could not recall the last time I had something new to wear—something that was not handed down from my brothers—and I felt my cup of happiness start to runneth over right there at the washbasin.

"I need help with this corset," I shouted into the big room. "I've seen something like it before, but I've never worn such a fancy, newfangled thing. I'm afraid it might strangle me."

"Stop that yelling—I'm right here," Aunt Kitty said, appearing behind me at the mirror. "I hardly live in a palace, Nell."

I could tell that Aunt Kitty's well of patience was not particularly deep, so I quickly began fastening the tiny front hooks before she could start yanking and tying the back laces.

"Not so tight," I heaved, after a particularly strong tug on the corset strings. "You'll crack my ribs!"

Aunt Kitty finished with the tying, then left to gather her bonnet and bag. I waited a few moments to catch my breath before facing the final layers of my dressing. As I slipped on the long camisole and the fresh-smelling petticoat, I noticed three more petticoats stacked right there on the bed, each embroidered more beautifully than the next. They were a dullish white from age, but that did not bother me one whit. I couldn't decide which I liked most. So I put them all on.

Heat or no, I was never, *ever* going to be mistaken for a boy again.

"There's a dress hanging on the wardrobe door," Aunt Kitty called. "Mrs. Wigginbottom passed it along to me, with those petticoats, too. Her washer girls outgrew them, so they are yours now."

I turned around and saw a red-and-white-checkered dress staring back at me. It was as ugly as a one-eyed dog, with long, faded sleeves and a collar at the top that probably had been white once. Now it was more the color of weak tea. The whole gown was about as worn out as an old dishrag, but I wasn't about to start complaining. It was the first dress I could call my own since, well . . . since my mama died.

Once I'd slipped into my boots and emerged from the bedroom, I had to bite my lip to keep from singing over the sheer joy of it all. Even though it was homely and ill-fitting, my dress nearly filled the doorframe. Aunt Kitty started up with her *tsk-tsk*ing as she fastened the row of buttons up the back, but I would have none of it. I was wearing petticoats for the first time that I could remember.

Puffed up proud like a rooster, I circled the room with my head held high. I knew I looked like a real, fashionable lady.

"Heavens" was what Aunt Kitty might have sighed just then as she watched me strut, my full skirts knocking over the umbrella stand. But I couldn't be sure, since it mixed with the sigh I was heaving at exactly the same time.

"Heavenly."

We eyed each other for a moment or two, and then we both headed for the staircase. This room was too hot for any more squabbling. Or strutting.

Chapter 5

In Which Aunt Kitty Visits a Detective Agency, and I Get Busy Snooping

We were on the street in minutes, and I didn't bother tying the sun hat's wide ribbon under my chin as I skipped after Aunt Kitty. Her ways outside were just as they were indoors—sharp and to the point. Her trim black boots made that familiar tip-tapping as she strode ahead down the wooden-plank sidewalk. And even though her knee might have been bothering her, there was no dawdling with Aunt Kitty.

"Where is it we're headed?" I asked, my voice a little breathy as I cantered beside her. There was a light wind off Lake Michigan, but it wasn't enough to cool an August day.

"I have business to attend to, down the block on Washington Street," she answered, darting behind a passing carriage as we weaved our way across a crowded street. "Mind that horse there, Nell."

I dodged the horse pulling a long omnibus on the center track. But I misjudged the steaming pile left behind by another of its kind. I was stomping it off my boot when Aunt Kitty began issuing me instructions.

"And when you wait outside, don't speak to a soul," she was saying over her shoulder as she trotted along, not even a drip of sweat on her brow. "I will be back downstairs as soon as I am finished."

Once my boot was scraped, I chased after her down the block. While she was still a pickled onion ready to drop me off at the nearest orphan home, there were moments when I found Aunt Kitty amazing. Like now, the way she was marching ahead as if she were going into battle, one long peacock feather flying proudly from her prim dark bonnet like a flag. Her hair was perfectly arranged, too, not a single strand daring to make its way out of place.

"Are you seeing a banker about your finances, Aunt Kitty?" I asked, dragging my left foot to clear the last bit of dung from my beloved boots. "Or maybe an attorney about tracking down more of our family? Or are you looking into real estate, maybe searching for a larger room to rent?"

"No, no, and no," she answered coolly, coming to a stop just before we reached a pair of wide wooden doors. She adjusted the shoulders of her blue jacket, then shook her skirt to loosen the dirt she'd collected on the walk. "I have no intention of telling you what I'm doing. Now wait here and don't budge an inch from this spot. I will not go scouring the city for a silly lost girl.

"And I've told you before, stop calling me Kitty. That may have been who I was in Chemung County. But here in Chicago I am Kate Warne."

She could say her name was Florence Nightingale, but she'd always be plain old Aunt Kitty to me. I wasn't about to go changing my thinking.

She left me there on the sidewalk and pushed on toward the big stone building's tall doors. I noticed the men gathered out front smoking cigars pulled off their hats as she approached. With quick nods and familiar greetings, one opened the door for her, and the other two stood a little straighter, wishing her a good day as she passed.

It was a curious sight, and I wondered what she was up to. Then, as she disappeared inside, I glanced at the sign painted on the front window. It read PINKERTON'S NATIONAL DETECTIVE AGENCY, and smack in the middle stared a wide, unblinking eye.

Underneath it were the words WE NEVER SLEEP.

That sounded like a good fit. Aunt Kitty didn't seem to sleep either. I'd heard her up last night, padding around the two rooms like a house cat and staring out at the moon. I figured she was worrying about money and food and whether she was going to keep me.

I hadn't slept much either.

Was Aunt Kitty in that building hiring herself a detective? Was she going to have someone search the whole country for a member of the Warne family stupid enough to take a hopeless, helpless girl? And what did a detective look like? I imagined a shadowy thug lurking in a corner saloon.

Kicking a rock into the street, I tried not to spit.

Aunt Kitty certainly was keen on getting rid of me the second she saw an opportunity. So my job was to make sure that opportunity never arose.

I fluffed up my weary checkered skirt, then leaned against the building for a while and watched life pass me by. More like I smelled it pass by, actually, what with the heat and the horses. First a dung cart rolled down the block, pulled by a scrawny brown horse that kept twitching its muscles to shoo the flies off its back. When a dairy wagon passed in the other direction, I watched the two beautiful white-footed dray horses that were pulling it.

That wagon stopped not ten paces away from me to make a milk delivery, so I decided to visit with the horses. Other than my family, there wasn't much I missed about Chemung County. But I did wish I could have brought my mule, Whiskey. I didn't know a thing about liquor when I named her. But I'd heard my daddy say whiskey was pure gold.

While I scratched the horse in front of me, I whispered a few sweet nothings into his ear and told him about Whiskey. His ear twitched a few times, letting me know he liked my story. Then I stepped over to his mate on the right and, just to be fair, gave this one a good scratching, too. When I came back around to the front of them, smiling and humming and stroking their muzzles, the one on the left gave me such a thank-you with his wide face, he knocked me flat on my hindquarters.

"Ha, ha! Watch out for the road apples! The dung cart missed a few!"

A newspaper boy was on the corner hawking his wares. He pointed at me sprawled out on Washington Street and doubled over laughing, slapping his knee like I was the funniest thing he'd ever seen. Boys were nothing but a pain in the neck, I mumbled, for my ears and those of the two horses. The one on the right let out a whinny of agreement.

I'd already taken a look at the *Chicago Press & Tribune* earlier today on Lake Street, during my rounds for Mrs. Wigginbottom. But this skinny newsboy had other papers in his arms that I hadn't read, and I wanted one of them to help me pass the time while I waited for my aunt.

"Care to make a trade?" I asked, pulling one of Mrs. Wigginbottom's rock-hard biscuits from under my bonnet. Papers cost two cents, and that was more money than I possessed in the world. But I could almost always get what I wanted in a barter.

I waved the biscuit under my nose and moaned, "*Mmmm*, fresh-baked."

This wasn't exactly lying—it had been fresh-baked about five days ago.

The newsboy was dough in my hands. In a blink, he pawed through the papers—the *Chicago Press & Tribune*, the *Galena Weekly North-Western Gazette*, and the *Amboy Times*—deciding which was meager enough to part with. I saw him lick his lips, so I knew he was as hungry as he looked.

"Here, take the *Amboy Times*," he said, his eyes on the biscuit as he shoved a paper at me. "Nobody reads them anymore, not since that abolitionist Abe Lincoln lost the Senate contest."

I slipped the paper under my arm and hurried off before he started making a fuss about cracking a tooth on that biscuit. Tucking into the shady doorway next to Pinkerton's, I perched myself on an empty wooden crate to have a read. The news was full of tragedies about train wrecks and grave robbers and wars being waged afar. I couldn't stop reading about the horrors—especially the stories about orphan asylums filled with unloved and underfed waifs. I turned the page and scanned past ads for saddlemakers, health tonics, even a billiard table.

Then I came across a story about that Lincoln man the newsboy mentioned. I'd never heard of Abraham Lincoln up in Chemung County.

"He is about six feet high, crooked-legged, stoop shouldered, spare built, and anything but handsome in the face," the paper said.

Having been called "anything but handsome" for most of my life, I felt a bit of kinship with this Mr. Lincoln.

"It is plain that nature took but little trouble in fashioning his outer man...As a close observer and cogent reasoner, he has few equals and perhaps no superior in the world," the reporter wrote. *"His language is pure and respectful, he attacks no man's character or motives, but fights with arguments."*

Fights with arguments! This Lincoln fellow was my kind of man.

I tore out the page on Mr. Lincoln and folded it up,

then poked it under my bonnet for safekeeping. The newsboy had called him an abolitionist. That rang a bell somewhere in my mind. I stared at my heavy brown boots and wiggled my toes in all the spare room I had in there. I'd heard my daddy called a lot of things these past few months since he died—most of them were uncharitable to his character—but the one that stuck in my mind was "abolitionist." I was going to have to keep reading if I wanted to figure out exactly what that meant.

It wasn't too much longer before Aunt Kitty emerged onto the sidewalk. She was talking with a big man whose bushy brown beard needed a good trimming. I wondered if that's what all detectives looked like.

"Excellent work, Mrs. Warne," he was saying, pumping my aunt's arm like he was trying to fill a water bucket. "Those ruffians are in jail, thanks to you. They never saw it coming." Though he might have been trying to keep his voice down, I could hear him plainly from where I sat. His accent was bouncy and strange, and I figured he must have come from somewhere exotic. Probably Texas.

When he disappeared back into the building, I jumped to my feet and onto the walkway beside my aunt, showering her with questions. I wanted to know what she was doing in there. Why was she visiting a detective agency? Was she trying more ways to rid herself of me? Where would she send me next?

Aunt Kitty let out a laugh and tugged on her dark gloves. "No, Nell, I am not hiring a detective to find more long-lost kin. Though that is a good idea."

She smoothed down her jacket and started that fast walking again. I kept up beside her this time. I had to know what my aunt was up to.

"Then what were you doing in there?" I pushed, even though it was clear Aunt Kitty did not want me poking around in her private affairs. "Are you a secretary for that Pinkerton? Or a bookkeeper?"

"No, Nell," she said, her voice tight. "I do not file his papers or keep his books. Nor do I take down Mr. Pinkerton's dictations."

I trailed behind her a few steps, my mind trying to sort things out.

"I know," I said with a skip, catching back up to

her. "Mrs. Wigginbottom said you help with the laundry and the sewing at the boardinghouse. Are you Mr. Pinkerton's washerwoman?"

"Washerwoman?" repeated Aunt Kitty, her body coming to a complete stop on the sidewalk. She glanced at the people pushing around us on either side, then she fixed her eyes on me—hard. Her voice was quiet when she spoke.

"I am not a washerwoman, Nell. I am not a secretary or a bookkeeper. For your information, I am a detective. In fact, I am the first woman Mr. Pinkerton has ever employed as such."

This news smacked me in the nose like a snowball in December. I stared up into her pretty face, at her high cheekbones and the way her hat sat on her head. She was every inch of her a lady.

"Why in the world would he do that?"

Aunt Kitty pounced on me as if I'd uttered a profanity right there on Washington Street for all to hear. Color rose up in her cheeks and turned them as red as radishes.

"Why would Mr. Pinkerton hire me, a woman? Because I can go where a man cannot—I can befriend the wives and girlfriends of criminals, and I can worm out their secrets. I can go where no one suspects me.

"And because I was not put on this earth to spend my days filing a man's papers or writing down every word he utters—nor washing trousers and darning his socks. Because I can do most any job a man can do, and maybe even do it better.

"I can do great things, Nell Warne. And so can you."

And she turned on her heel and started with more of that fast, tip-tap walking, her shoulders square and tall like she was Queen Victoria all over again.

I let out a *whoop-di-dee* and skipped along behind her, and Aunt Kitty didn't even bother to shush me. The smile I saw in the corner of her eyes told me she felt the same way.

Chapter 6

In Which Jemma Recalls an Old Goat

September 17, 1859

Dear Cornie,

Mama and me are sorry to hear about your daddy passing away. It's gotten me to thinking about him and my papa and our days in Chemung County. Even though your daddy was not a shining example of Christian virtue, I recall he was still a good man. I remember that Christmas when he gave you the goat you named Daffodil. When your mama learned he'd won it in a poker match, she was angry as a hornet. But you loved Daffodil so much, nobody could take that goat away from you.

It used to be that Mama checked every one of my letters to you. She doesn't want us saying anything about your daddy's business or what happened to your family. Or to mine. Mama worries all the time, saying lots of folks could get into trouble if we say too much, if we write down names and places.

She doesn't talk about it, but something bad happened to Mama's friend a few years back. Down South—in Georgia, I believe it was. Mama and her friend were writing letters about folks who were running to freedom here in Canada. And the next thing Mama knows, her friend's neck is in a noose hanging from a tree.

She says it was the letters to blame. Someone read them who shouldn't have.

Mama doesn't have time to check my letters anymore now that the babies are a handful. But we should use a cipher, just in case. Like writing

1 for A, 2 for B, on through the alphabet.
Or secret names and such. That way nobody
but us will understand who we're talking about.
Just use your imagination, and I will do the
same.

Mama and the babies are fine, but I miss the
dear Maple Tree. He's been moving around from
place to place these past few years. Mama's so
afraid for him staying safe from harm. But I will
tell you this. He never did settle down here in
Saint Catharines with us. The Maple Tree is a
conductor in a big city now. We only hear word
about him now and again from folks who make it
through.

I wonder if you might get news of him. You
must tell me if you do, please. Do you still
keep up with the papers? Mama's not one for
listening to gossip, but that's the only way I
know what's going on. I say gossip is just like a
newspaper, only written in whispers instead of
ink. Sure you can't always believe everything
you hear, but isn't that the same with the
newspaper?

I am praying this letter finds you good, and that the Right Reverend was able to track down your long-lost kin in Chicago. I hope it's a rich old granny who wants to spoil you silly. And that she has lots of family there— then you'll never be alone again.

My candle's burning out. I will write later.

Your friend forever and ever,
Jemma

Chapter 7

In Which I Encounter a Seventh Daughter of a Seventh Daughter

I t was a few weeks later when fall swept into town, turning the air crisp and cool. The whole city of Chicago seemed suddenly to overflow with orange pumpkins and tart apples. I was munching on a bright red one I'd picked up during my afternoon marketing when I came across an advertisement in the newspaper that made me jump out of my chair.

"Did you read this, Aunt Kitty?" I hollered, though she was only an arm's length away, seated at the small table by the window. She was grinding coffee beans in a wooden box—another of the many tasks performed for Mrs. Wigginbottom and the rent. "The newspaper says there's a fortune-teller in town! Says she's the Seventh Daughter of a Seventh Daughter. Madam L. L. Lucille's her name."

My aunt turned the long metal handle of the coffee grinder and stared at me. The coffee's aroma was strong and comforting, and I had to fight the urge to sneak downstairs into Mrs. Wigginbottom's kitchen and pour myself another cup.

"She'll tell who loves you, who hates you," I read breathlessly from the newspaper page, "and your future husband."

I stood there waiting for Aunt Kitty to grab her bag and head for the door. If anybody was due for a husband to magically appear out of thin air, it was my soon-to-be-matronly aunt. But there she sat, grinding her bitter coffee and giving me a blank look like I was speaking Egyptian. I urged her on a few more times.

"I know, Nell," she said calmly. "I'm already aware of Madam Lucille and her Powerful, All-Seeing Eye."

"Well, what are we waiting for? Let's get a move on. We've got fortunes to claim."

But Aunt Kitty sat there perched like a pigeon on

a park bench. Maybe she already knew about the cost of one of Madam Lucille's readings—at ten dollars per session and two of us needing our futures revealed, well, that wasn't difficult arithmetic.

"Is the cost too dear?" I asked, slipping into the chair across from her. "Perhaps Mr. Pinkerton could give you a raise."

She shook her head and peeked at the ground coffee.

"Afraid of romance?" I followed.

She let out a choking cough.

"Something you're hiding in your past?"

She set the grinder down on the table and sent a deep sigh into the air.

"Get ahold of yourself, Nell," she began, tapping the freshly ground beans into a big black tin. "You don't really believe in fortune-telling, now do you?"

Jumping Jehoshaphat, of course I did! And she'd be wise to try to read up on the power of the stars as well. Not all learning about life could be found in books. One look into the night sky, and a true believer could glimpse the turning wheel of Destiny.

"Why do you ask?" I hedged. "Don't you believe in mystics, Aunt Kitty?"

She scoffed and stepped over to the fireplace, setting the black coffee tin on the mantel. We would take it downstairs to Mrs. Wigginbottom at supper.

"I don't believe one whit in such shams, nor should you, Nell Warne."

"Why not? Madam Lucille could lead you to love again—to a life of happiness and riches. Why would you not trust her to reveal Life's Wondrous Plan?"

"Because, foolish girl," she huffed, turning around from the fireplace with a devilish grin, "I am Madam Lucille herself."

I had just risen to my feet, but this news sent me staggering back into my chair like I was punched. Aunt Kitty was Madam Lucille, the Great Mystic?

"You're a Seventh Daughter of a Seventh Daughter...?"

"Goodness, no, Nell! It's part of our latest case. I will be playing the role of a fortune-teller in order to solve another mystery."

I couldn't believe she was letting on about one of her cases. I asked her whether it was another instance of jewelry theft—there had been lots of stories in the newspaper about that. But she shook her head and gave me a solemn look, like she was sizing up what sort of information I could handle. With all her comings and goings the past few weeks, she'd never yet shared a word about her detective work.

"I only tell you this much because I could use your help sewing costumes," she said. "We will have marvelous disguises."

I felt peevish that she didn't trust me enough to share more. She must have thought I'd go jabbering all over town about her private business.

"Fine, don't tell me what you're up to," I said with a huffy breath. Then I mumbled for my ears alone, "Sounds like a bunch of grown-up persons running around playing make-believe."

However, my ears were not the only ones to have heard.

"Playing make-believe?" said Aunt Kitty with an icy edge. "You think that's what we're doing? Perhaps I should let you know the seriousness of our work. How does catching a ruthless man trying to murder his wife sound to you, Nell? Murder by poison—slow and agonizing."

Murder? I wondered how dressing up as a mystic

would solve a mystery like this one. So she explained a bit, how a sea captain had come into Mr. Pinkerton's office in a fit of worry. His sister had fallen in love with a bad man. He suspected the bad man was trying to kill off his wife in order to be with the sea captain's sister.

"Because the sister is so superstitious, Mr. Pinkerton believes we can get her to reveal the secrets to this murder scheme," Aunt Kitty said. "And, he hopes, we can save her from making a terrible mistake."

Aunt Kitty pulled a few handbills from her bag and handed one to me. She said Mr. Pinkerton's operatives would be passing them out on the street where the sea captain's sister lives. Between these and the newspaper advertisement, the detectives were hoping to snare the sister in their trap.

I ran my fingers across the handbill. It was the same advertisement for Madam Lucille, the All-Seeing Mystic, that I'd seen in the newspaper. My eyes lingered longingly over the promise to reveal our fortunes. Did mine lie in detective work, like Aunt Kitty? In nursing soldiers back to health, like Florence Nightingale? I'd read all about her heroic exploits in the newspaper.

I imagined that my Destiny might be in roving the land as a keen-eyed journalist—recording history's most exhilarating moments as they unfurled before my very eyes. All while wearing smart dresses and fashionable bonnets, of course. Now, there was the life.

I let out a heavy sigh. Those secrets would be left in the hands of Fate now.

"And Nell," my aunt began, her eyes watching me fold the handbill and slip it into the pocket of my checkered dress, "you know better. I have but one husband, Matthew, and he was killed when your father—"

"My father didn't kill your Matthew in anger, Aunt Kitty," I interrupted, rising to my feet once again. "It was an accident."

"Where is your proof, Nell?" Her voice was sharp as we faced off across the table. "How can you stand before me and assert such a thing? The Cornelius Warne I knew was a liar, a drinker, and a poker-playing cheat. He probably shot my Matthew over money or liquor."

And then she paused, taking a deep breath to collect herself. She started up again, more softly.

"Your head is full of stories that your family made up, Nell, stories to help a little girl fall asleep at night. There is no truth to them."

"That family is your family, too, Aunt Kitty."

"No, it is not. And stop calling me Kitty. You're holding on to something that doesn't exist anymore, to someone I was a long time ago. I am Kate Warne now, with a life and a job that has nothing to do with Chemung County. I'm not Kitty."

A house divided, that's what we were: both of us a Warne, but each of us seeing things differently. The questions about my daddy cut like a raging river between us, threatening to tear us apart.

I'd read in the newspaper about Mr. Lincoln saying the same thing in a speech to folks in Ohio: *"A house divided against itself cannot stand."* He was quoting a Bible verse that I knew by heart. Only Mr. Lincoln was talking about slavery splitting the whole country in two—*"I believe this government cannot endure permanently half slave and half free."*

I stared hard into Aunt Kitty's pinched, pickled-onion face and wondered about the two of us. Would we endure?

Chapter 8

In Which Aunt Kitty Introduces Madam Lucille, and I Meet a Superstitious Sister and a Boy

We were wandering around Mr. Potter Palmer's dry-goods store just a day or so later, my fingers aching from working so many hours on Aunt Kitty's red fortune-teller costume. We had already spent the morning at an auction, where she bought up exotic trinkets to use in her charade as Madam L. L. Lucille. I had never witnessed such haggling over prices. My aunt seemed to hate parting with those crisp bills she pulled from a special purse that George Bangs, the Pinkerton office manager, had supplied to cover expenses. Now she was venturing upstairs to the fabric department to haggle over bolts of cloth for another costume.

I headed for my favorite display case to study the earrings, necklaces, and rings. While me and Aunt Kitty had cooled off from our disagreement about my daddy, I did not want to push my luck by staying in her company for too many hours at a time.

"The smell is particularly wretched today," declared a pretty, blond lady, pressing a lace hankie to her nose to keep the stench away. "Must be the wind."

Chicago was never too fragrant to begin with. Between the animal carcasses floating in the river, the deep pools of mud on the streets, and the factories puffing long plumes of stink into the air, this place was no garden party for the senses. And Mr. Potter Palmer had unfortunately situated his store just steps from the Chicago River, where all the city's dirt, death, and decay bobbed along on the current.

"Smells a bit like horse," I volunteered, eager to share my knowledge of the city's finer points. I'd read lots of stories about the trains barreling through Chicago—"More than a hundred a day!" boasted the newspapers—and the hazards they posed for anything in their way. "I think a whiff of what the train hit yesterday is riding on the breeze today."

I was beaming at the salesclerk and the pretty lady, proud that I was able to share a few bits of current events. But he just gave his throat a loud clearing. And the pretty lady looked like she needed a bucket.

Maybe they were not as interested in current events as I had presumed.

She moved along looking at the jewels, and I moved along, too. We crisscrossed our paths as we circled the viewing cases, our eyes dancing over the gold and silver, the pearls and rubies and sapphires.

"That opal there looks like it's lit from within," I whispered solemnly, as if we were in church. The Potter Palmer & Co. emporium did inspire a sense of reverence in me whenever I stepped inside. "It almost seems like a magic stone."

"I do believe opals have the magic power," came the pretty lady's breathy reply. "My brother wears one in a ring. And as he's a sea captain, the opal forewarns him of ocean storms. He says it has never been wrong."

I stared at the opal ring and imagined it on my finger, giving me the All-Seeing Eye like Madam Lucille.

Make that plain old Aunt Kitty, I reminded myself. How I longed to have it. But that ring cost a fortune, and it didn't require much talent in arithmetic to know that I couldn't afford it.

"Where did your brother get his magic ring?" I inquired.

And just like that, the pretty lady—Mrs. Annie Thayer was her name, I quickly learned—told me the whole tale about how her father received three opal rings from a powerful guru during his sailing days.

"The first is buried with Papa, the second went to the grave with Mama, and the third adorns my brother's hand. But I desperately want it for myself."

Her story was so full of superstition, I felt right away that we were kindred spirits. We could have been sisters, Mrs. Thayer and me. Although her colorful blue eyes and long yellow curls were in sharp contrast to my murky brown peepers and cropped, coffee-colored hair.

"If only my brother would let me have it," Mrs. Thayer whispered, stepping closer to me over the jewelry case like we were old pals. I noticed the sales-clerk didn't want to miss a word either, so he leaned his ear over toward us as he polished the glass. "That ring would give me the power to win over my true love. He has a wife, but his heart belongs to me alone."

Suddenly something clicked in my mind.

Her brother was a sea captain.

She was as superstitious as a black cat breaking a mirror in a graveyard.

Her true love had a wife.

I reached into the pocket of my checkered dress and pulled out the handbill Aunt Kitty had given me the other day.

"Here's something you might consider," I said, unfolding the advertisement and smoothing down the creases. The salesclerk stopped his polishing altogether now, and he pressed in close beside Mrs. Thayer to have a see. "Have you ever heard of the world-famous mystic, Madam L. L. Lucille? She's the Seventh Daughter of a Seventh Daughter..."

The next morning I awoke to find Aunt Kitty in a frenzy of activity. The finished costume of rich red silk lay across her bed, and she was busy draping reams of sunny yellow material across the foot of mine.

"Get moving as quickly as you can, Nell," she ordered, pinching a few stickpins between her lips as she hurriedly tried to hem a pair of black pants. How much coffee had she drunk already? The morning sky peeking through our curtain was still pink and new, but she looked as if her workday were nearly finished. "Mr. Pinkerton rented a room for the fortune-telling over on Clark Street. We need to be set up in just a few hours."

There would be no time for marketing, and Mrs. Wigginbottom was not happy with this news. I vowed to work doubly hard the next day, but she took little consolation in that promise, showering me with complaints as heavy as hailstones as I rushed out the kitchen door.

By the time we covered the walls and windows of the Clark Street room with dark fabrics and draperies, nary a ray of sunlight could penetrate inside. I helped Aunt Kitty place a tall mirror at the far end of the room, which created a dizzying appearance of there being two rooms. We set skeletons on either side of the mirror to stand sentry. They looked to me like guardians to the underworld. With a little help from some of the other operatives, we hung five silver lamps around the room—one in each of the four corners, and the fifth hanging in the very center. Light from these ornate lanterns gave the room a hazy yellow glow, and thick, noxious incense filled my nose and stung my eyes.

We dragged a large chair and a lounge to the center of the room, placing them before Madam Lucille's low table. On the table itself, we decided on just two things: a large globe and a star chart for easy consultation with the Big Dipper and the North Star.

"Nell, I wonder if you'd be willing to help me even more today," Aunt Kitty said, studying my face with a somber expression. She was probably thinking about our last disagreement, and how divided the Warne house currently was.

"One of the boys is sick, and he was to work the front room. Our charade is ruined if we don't find someone to replace him."

Aunt Kitty wanted my help? Doing real detective work?

She didn't have to ask twice.

"Where do I change my clothes?" I said.

Her face went soft for a moment, and I knew she was grateful to see I wasn't holding a grudge. "Hurry now, Nell, our door opens at ten sharp!"

She handed me a costume, and I dove behind the bright yellow curtain I'd just helped hang. I was to portray a Turkish boy in baggy black pants and a white cotton shirt. I put my arms through a fitted red vest that looked strangely familiar: I'd seen Aunt Kitty sewing on this vest over the past weeks, making it out of an old shawl she'd found left behind by one of Mrs. Wigginbottom's quarrelsome tenants.

I sniffed at each shoulder and smelled the familiar boiled-cabbage odor of our boardinghouse. Aunt Kitty liked to save a dime where she could, and I imagined that Mr. Bangs, the office manager, appreciated that. But while her frugal ways were impressive, they were also sour-smelling.

I tugged my boots on and tucked the ballooning black fabric into the tops. Then I found a basin of water and slicked back my hair from my face, topping it off with a bright red fez. When I passed the mirror,

I hardly recognized my own reflection. I stood mesmerized by the brown-eyed boy staring back at me.

He looked perfectly exotic.

Except he had enormous ears.

"Excuse me, son," mumbled the same sturdy-looking gentleman who had helped us with the lanterns. He was pushing past me with a heavy candlestick in his arms.

"Detective, that's not a boy," said my aunt, laughing. "That's my niece! Nell Warne, I'd like you to meet the sharp-eyed Detective Timothy Webster."

We shook hands in a sort of playful formal introduction. And I didn't even mind that I'd been mistaken for a boy again. This time, it was in the line of duty. As if to test my hardiness, Detective Webster gave my hand a painful squeeze. So I squeezed his hand right back. He wouldn't let go, so I decided I wouldn't either. And there we stood for a few silent seconds, locked in a jaw-clenching standoff until our eyes began to tear up. I imagine his were more from wanting to laugh, while mine were from the agony of his brawny hand.

Aunt Kitty, however, was the real sight for our watery eyes. When she stepped from behind the bright yellow curtain, which also hid a secret office, she looked as if she'd just walked out of a pyramid in the desert. Her face and hands were rubbed with olive oil and shone with radiance. Her hair, which she usually wore twisted into a neat bun, was hanging in heavy masses to her waist. The sleeves of her deep red dress were bell-shaped and flowing, the rich fabric embellished with golden trim. And her skirt had endless petticoats beneath it, trailing behind her more than a yard when she drifted gracefully through the room. Oh, how I admired that dress!

"Nell, you are to go by the name Ali from hence forward. When I ring the bell, you are to usher our visitors in or out. Do you understand?"

I nodded silently, too scared of this Apostle of the Occult to call forth my voice, and headed for the door. I bowed deeply as the first customers arrived, taking their ten dollars and slipping the cash deep into my pants pockets to save for Mr. Pinkerton. I was busy for a good forty-five minutes before something important happened.

Chapter 9

In Which I Am All Ears

The door to the fortune-telling salon opened, and in walked Mrs. Annie Thayer, the pretty lady from Mr. Potter Palmer's emporium, seeking a consultation with Madam Lucille. I knew she did not recognize me, as she referred to me as "young man." So I hurriedly showed her to a seat in the waiting area and raced into Aunt Kitty's room, giving her the signal to come meet me behind the yellow curtain—fast.

"Ali, what are you thinking?" she snapped, looking all the more terrifying with her eyes burning at me. "You cannot interrupt me when I am with a customer."

"It's important, Aunt Kitty!"

"Madam Lucille," she corrected, her eyes darting back toward the salon. My aunt was a stickler for staying in character lest we were overheard, even when the only creatures nearby that could possibly do any overhearing were the skeletons at the back of the room and a few stray mice. "Now, what is it?"

I told her about the pretty lady and her superstitious beliefs surrounding her brother's opal ring.

"What did you say her name was?" Aunt Kitty asked eagerly.

"Mrs. Annie Thayer. Is that the lady you're seeking?"

Aunt Kitty clapped her hands and gave me such a look of pride, I felt a flower start to blossom in my chest.

"Indeed! Annie Thayer is our quarry," she whispered gleefully. "It is her lover we are after, but Mr. Pinkerton believes she will deliver him."

I told her everything I could recall of our conversation about the opal ring—things Mrs. Thayer told me directly and things that were sort of hinted at: her mother and father must be dead, I explained, since she said two rings were buried with them. She said her brother's ring warned him of storms at sea, so maybe she believed other things could predict the future.

"This is perfect," Aunt Kitty said softly, leaning in close to study my face. "We were trying to lure her here, and now you've delivered her. How did you find out so much about her, Nell?"

"I'm Ali, remember?" I corrected, and we both smiled. Then I felt embarrassed that she was making a fuss. I wasn't used to her being soft on me like this. "Folks like to talk about themselves, I suppose. And when they find a listener, they keep on jabbering. Plus, it don't—er, *doesn't*—hurt to be blessed with a good set of ears."

"That you have," she said, giving my right one a quick tug. Then she sailed back to her low table and quickly got rid of the fortune seeker who was there.

"Poor motherless child!" Madam Lucille exclaimed a few minutes later, as I escorted Mrs. Thayer into the hazy salon. Mrs. Thayer gave a start and flung herself into the large chair in front of my aunt's table as if surrendering. "Still yourself, you poor motherless child!"

76

"H-how did you know my mother is gone?" stuttered Mrs. Thayer.

"I am a seer of Yesterday, Today, and Tomorrow," replied Madam Lucille spookily. "Of Good"—then she dropped her voice to a throaty whisper—"and Evil."

Mrs. Thayer shuddered.

"I see three men in your life," continued Madam Lucille, rolling her eyes back into her head and running her hands over the smooth globe. "One is your Past, one is your Present, and one"—she did that same dramatic hush—"is your Future."

"Go on," gasped Mrs. Thayer, looking pale but sitting on the edge of her seat now.

"The first man is far away, perhaps a traveler," Madam Lucille began. "I see water now—he is a sailor. And he loves you dearly. Is he family? Yes, yes he is. I think he is . . . your brother!"

And so the all-seeing Madam Lucille revealed her mystical eye to Mrs. Thayer for what felt like an eternity. And even though I knew the ins and outs of such hokum, I was still impressed. Finally, Madam Lucille said she was exhausted by all the charting of stars and consulting of the zodiac around the Past. So she told Mrs. Thayer to return tomorrow in order to clear the mists around her Present and Future.

As I escorted the woozy client through the waiting room and out the door, I felt an itch of guilt begin to bother my conscience like a mosquito bite. It seemed wrong to work Mrs. Thayer up into a lather like this.

What had she done that was so bad to justify misleading her as we were?

"Murder," Aunt Kitty answered later that day, as she shimmied out of her scarlet gown in the back room. "The deed is done. Her lover has succeeded in putting his wife in a pine box."

I was agog. The fresh-faced blond woman, with cheeks as delicate as a china doll's, was in cahoots with a killer? I sat down at the fortune-teller table and let out a heavy sigh. Keeping track of Good and Evil was exhausting, especially when Evil looked like such a respectable person. While that lover sounded horrible indeed, if Mrs. Annie Thayer knew what he was up to, she was just as fiendish.

Mrs. Thayer returned two more times in the following days—to have her Present and Future read.

And both times she was put into a frenzy by Madam Lucille's All-Seeing Eye turning up the secrets of her private life. But it no longer irritated my conscience.

"I see danger in your Present," my aunt boomed, both her acting and her disguise making her appear every bit a true mystic. "Danger! There is a man who lurks in the shadows. He is not alone; he is with another. It is a woman, yes. I think I see a woman beside him."

"Is it my lover and me?" asked Mrs. Thayer thickly. I could have smacked my forehead over her blind stupidity, but I held myself in check.

Madam Lucille thundered on as if she hadn't heard the question.

"This woman, she is in a swirling mist. She is fading in and out, hovering between life and death. I see her grasping, begging—she doesn't want to leave us. Wait!" And here Madam Lucille gasped and looked away as if she couldn't bear to speak.

"What is it? Do go on, Madam Lucille!"

"She is going, going, gone. The woman is"—and here my aunt paused for a few dramatic seconds—"dead."

Mrs. Thayer fell back in her chair, her head lolling on the pillow as if she were a rag doll. Clasping my

Turkish fez to my head, I raced out of the room to fetch a glass of water. That was all she could take of the second day's meeting.

But on the third, she seemed resigned to her Destiny. She sat rigid in the large chair before Madam Lucille and steeled herself for what was to come.

"The third man," began my mystical aunt, her hands gliding over the globe on her table, "he is your Future."

"I must know," whispered Mrs. Thayer urgently, "will he marry me?"

Again I had to suppress the urge to roll my eyes at this woman's senseless pursuit of a husband. Could she hear no higher calling than the wedding chapel?

"No, he is a stranger to you. But you are to trust him," Madam Lucille said coolly. "If you follow his advice, this handsome stranger can save you from harm."

Mrs. Thayer asked how she would know him.

"It will seem at first as an ordinary encounter. But you will soon see his wisdom, for he urgently wants to talk with you. His eyes are gray, his cheeks ruddy. His hair is brown, and his beard is full. His manner of speech sounds exotic. He knows about your Past and Present, and if you allow, he can influence your Future.

"I see again this man of your Past. He is the man who loves you—your brother. He wishes to save you from punishment. I see the man of your Present. He is the one you call your lover. But what's this? I see a net around him, as if he is being caught. The ghost of his wife hovers over the scene, desperately whispering the word *poison*."

Mrs. Thayer swooned but stayed upright, gripping the arm of the chair with white knuckles and staring wildly at Madam Lucille.

"You are also in danger of the net," she whispered into Mrs. Thayer's ashen face. "Only the truth can set you free."

Annie Thayer left so hastily, I ran to the window to watch her make her way through the Clark Street crowd down below us. Just as she reached the corner, I saw her meet a man with a ruddy complexion and brown hair, full whiskers on his face—though I would not describe him as "handsome" by any stretch of my imagination.

"That's Mr. Pinkerton she's talking to down there!"

I shouted to my aunt, who seemed to take the news without the least bit of surprise.

I learned later that Mrs. Thayer sat down with this third man of her Future at his detective agency, and she provided a full confession about her lover's wicked deed. Detective work seemed to me to be two parts costuming and one part luck.

Chapter 10

※❦❦❦❦❧❦❦❦❦※

In Which I Explain the Pickled Onion

November 2, 1859

Dear Jemma,

It might sound harsh to describe my kin as such, but Pickled Onion best sums up her character. She is strong and bracing, and she occasionally brings tears to my eyes. Like just the other day, when we came across another tenant's castoffs. She held open her bag and had me scoop them up like we were at a fashion emporium!

I protested, but she just saw that trash as treasure.

Sometimes I believe she needs spectacles.

"I can use the pheasant feathers off that hat to dress up an old bonnet of mine," she told me. Then she said with such a tone, "Frugality is a virtue. It says so in the Bible."

Well, you know we owned one book back at our house in Chemung County—the Holy Bible written by Mr. King James himself. You read it as much as I did. So I told the Pickled Onion it says no such thing about the Good Lord smiling on the cheap.

Well that got her back up. "I am not cheap," she declared. "I am frugal. There is a difference." I told her she was talking like some churchgoing know-it-all when she ain't one. Well, what do you think she said back to me?

"Aren't. Mind your grammar."

Then she went on telling me I couldn't convince her that my whiskey-loving, poker-playing, so-and-so of a father took me to Sunday school each week. That cut me to the bone. So I warned her that she ought not to bring up my daddy anymore. I think she understood.

When we disagree like that, I worry that she'll pack my bag and drop me off at the nearest orphan asylum. She don't trust me, and I don't trust her, so I guess in that sense we are even. One good thing about the Pickled Onion is her employment, which I cannot tell you about.

I will share this, though I know better about such things. I believe she has a special power! It is very possible the Pickled Onion is able to

18 5 1 4 / 20 8 5 / 19 20 1 18 19!

I hope you can figure that out. In the meantime, I must learn more about the night her husband died. I was so young, I don't recall the particulars of it. And I fear that I remind the Pickled Onion of his passing. When she looks at my face, she sees my daddy's. And all she thinks about is the part he played in that tragedy. She seems to believe I share my daddy's same vices—that I might take up with the gambling, whiskey, and general rapscallionism.

I am sorry the Maple Tree's job as a conductor takes him so far away. I know he must miss you and the others something awful. When did he start working for the railroads? Here's something I can tell to you straight. I read a story that they're testing a new railroad car fit for sleeping in, called a Pullman. They're making them here in Chicago. Perhaps the Maple Tree will get to ride in one of those!

Could you give me a cipher and let me know how to reach him?

Very truly your friend,
Cornie (but I go by Nell now)

Chapter 11

In Which I Fall Victim to the Silent Sit

We're signing you up for school today," Aunt Kitty announced one chilly winter morning. "The Home for the Friendless currently offers no educational enrichment. So until we find the proper arrangement for you, Nell, we must get you back to your lessons. An uneducated girl is worse than a lame horse."

This news sent my needle poking into my finger. I let out an angry yelp.

"Where did you hear that bit of wisdom?" I asked, dropping the petticoat beside my rocking chair and getting to my feet. "Just because a girl don't go to school don't mean she's not educated. You see how many newspapers I read."

"*Doesn't*," she corrected in that tight, pickled-onion way. "And while you were quick-thinking on the fortune-teller case and I have observed you are a strong reader, your grammar and arithmetic skills leave much to be desired."

Not much of what Aunt Kitty was saying appealed to me. But the words that rattled my ears most were *until we find the proper arrangement for you*. She was still planning to ship me off somewhere! Even though I was mindful to stay busy and be a help to her, it was clear I had more work to do to earn my keep. Aunt Kitty might not have been knocking at the orphan asylum's doors this time, but school?

I begged her not to make me go.

Pacing back and forth between our chairs, I promised to stay up nights drilling my sums and improving my vocabulary. But she only complained that I'd burn up all the lamp oil, which would drive up our debt to Mrs. Wigginbottom again.

"School," she repeated. "You need the firm hand of a schoolmarm, Nell. We will enroll you today."

She sounded determined. It was time to take drastic measures.

"Aunt Kitty," I began, trying out her same cool delivery just to see how it would go over, "these schools here in Chicago have seventy, maybe one hundred kids in each classroom. If you make me go, I'll catch the croup and die before Christmas."

She did not look moved.

"Or I might pick up foul language and rough habits."

She merely cleared her throat and dusted at her sleeve.

I was not getting through.

"Or even worse," I whispered, watching her lean in a bit closer to hear me. "Head lice."

Aunt Kitty gasped and shot both hands to her tidy brown hair.

Conversation over. I would take my lessons at home.

"But you will mind my instruction," she ordered,

smoothing her fingers over her tightly braided bun. "And you will work each evening, before sundown, to finish your vocabulary lessons and the fundamentals of arithmetic."

I assured her I would. And feeling a bit smug over my victory, I returned to my rocking chair and pulled the petticoat back onto my lap. Making sure to keep the smile from my face, I resumed my sewing, though I couldn't keep my toes from giving a vigorous push to that rocking chair.

We sat in silence for a bit, the only sound the *creak-cruck* of my chair. Once I finally got the needle threaded, I was ready to start hemming again. I scratched at a scar on my hand and felt Aunt Kitty's eyes watching me.

"Where did you get that?" she asked, nodding at the heart-shaped welt on my right hand. I slipped it under the edge of the dingy petticoat, trying to hide the ugly pink mark from her detection. But it was too late. And now she wanted me to talk about it.

If I'd learned anything from Aunt Kitty, it was the art of the Silent Sit. Just ask someone a question and then sit there, as quiet as a stone. Most folks can't take silence for more than a few ticks on the clock, and they start trying to fill it like an empty bucket. I knew Aunt Kitty was using her tricks on me, but I always seemed to fall for them.

"It's nothing," I said, wishing she didn't take notice of every little thing. Then, to fill the quiet, I added, "Just a reminder of Chemung County."

"Is it a burn?"

It was and it wasn't. I peeked over at her face, which was patiently waiting for me to talk. I pinched my lips tight, but it was no use.

"I got blistered," I explained, a little self-conscious about the ugly welt. "But not from tending the hearth or lighting a lamp. It comes from my gun misfiring."

Aunt Kitty's eyebrows arched. She seemed surprised to hear that I used a weapon back on the farm. But how did she think food got on the table? That it walked right up onto our plates and lay down beside the cornbread?

"After Mama died, my daddy left us for a while," I said, mindful not to tell her too much, lest she go and use it against me sometime. But she was sitting there so silent, my mouth started running on and on just to fill up all the quiet. "My brothers, Zeke and Jeremiah, took over the farming, which left me to care for everything else. That meant putting supper in the pot each day. Rabbit, squirrel, possum, muskrat. You name it. I got to be a pretty good shot."

Aunt Kitty stopped asking me questions—didn't even say a word about my daddy leaving us kids all alone. Instead she just sat across from me in her deep blue parlor chair and stared at my scar peeking out beneath the petticoat.

I bit my bottom lip to keep from chattering any more. I wasn't going to let her Silent Sit get the better of me. But I could tell something I'd said about my scar or my gun had gotten her to thinking.

"Did you receive a new letter from your friend Jemma?" she finally asked, getting up to dust the fireplace mantel. Aunt Kitty never wasted a minute on rest and relaxation. Not when a dust mite could be lurking in her midst. "The way you put it away whenever I enter the room—you seem secretive about her."

It wasn't easy living with a detective. Certain things I wanted to keep in the shadows had a way of being drawn out into the open for casual discussion.

"No secrets," I said vaguely, hoping she'd leave it at that. "Just some private research is all."

But my aunt wasn't one for leaving things well enough alone.

"Where did you say this Jemma lives? I don't recall hearing you mention her people...."

I paused, shouting inside my head to keep my mouth shut. But I couldn't help it. The room had grown quiet, and I could hear the clock on the fireplace mantle quietly mark the passing of time.

"Jemma Tuthill's her name," I said, kicking myself for divulging that bit of information. I paused, but that Silent Sit got me again. "Her people come from up in Chemung County, like us. She doesn't live there no more—*anymore*—but she used to when we were girls. She's safe in Canada now."

Aunt Kitty turned from wiping down the wooden table by the window and looked at me. "That's nice" was all she said.

I looked at her suspiciously. Now I was on her trail! Aunt Kitty didn't utter meaningless comments like "That's nice" unless her thoughts were racing off somewhere else.

I knew she recognized the Tuthill name.

"Didn't you know her people when you lived there?" I asked casually, pushing back and forth in my rocking chair again. "They lived close to us Warnes."

Aunt Kitty picked up her sewing project and began folding it into a neat pile. She laid the red skirt from her fortune-teller costume into her basket, along with some pretty plaid material she was reworking into a new gown. She pretended to be deeply interested in her fabrics.

"Might have," she said quickly.

A little too quickly, I noted.

"The Tuthills were free black folks who lived on the other side of our neighbor's property. Do you recall? Jemma's daddy was friends with my daddy. And since Jemma was my age, we were always together."

"Nell, you know I left when you were no more than seven—"

"Eight," I corrected.

"Around the time of the—"

"—accident," I interrupted.

We stared into each other's faces a moment or two.

I told Aunt Kitty a little about Jemma, how she

wasn't allowed to go to school with me. So every night we'd hole up in the hayloft, and we'd play school. That's how Jemma learned everything that I did. And maybe even better, since she had a way with writing her ABCs and I couldn't care less about swoops and curlicues back then.

Aunt Kitty gave me a disapproving scowl, and I pushed on before she brought up adding penmanship to my lessons in vocabulary and sums.

"Before long, some bad things started happening. Jemma and me were on Whiskey's back, fetching seed from the store for my daddy, when we saw it ourselves. White men were riding into town and rounding up black folks. Saying something about runaway slaves.

"I remember the way Jemma started shaking. The day was warm, but her body was trembling like it was January. Her kin weren't runaways or fugitives— Daddy said they'd been farming Chemung County dirt as long as us Warnes. But that didn't matter."

I paused, letting my words catch up to my thinking. I still missed Jemma so much. And while I knew with certainty I'd never see my family again, I couldn't help but hang on to the hope that someday I'd see Jemma.

"Not long after that day, Jemma and her family left. They fled Chemung County in the dead of night. My brothers said they had to go find freedom somewhere else."

Aunt Kitty stepped over to the window like she was done listening. I knew she didn't like to bring up the past—anything to do with Chemung County had to do with her Matthew.

And his dying.

The wooden floorboards creaked beneath her as she paced around the room. She stopped now and then to straighten a book or align the curtains.

"How?" Aunt Kitty asked quietly. "How did Jemma Tuthill and her family get to freedom? Do you know?"

"She's only starting to tell me the details—" I began, catching myself. I'd been too young to understand when it all happened. But now that I was living with Aunt Kitty, well, I was doing my own detective work.

"Jemma won't risk revealing anyone's name in case our letters get opened. So we're using a secret code. Some folks call it a cipher. We're protecting the innocent."

"The innocent?" scoffed Aunt Kitty, more for her ears than mine. She spat into her dustrag and began polishing the window. But I could still hear her muttering to herself. "I imagine those letters aren't about Cornelius Warne. Because *innocent* is not a word to be associated with him."

I jumped to my feet, my boots making a hollow clomping noise on the floor. The echoes from Chemung County hung in the air between us.

Aunt Kitty set her dustrag on the table and went to fetch her bonnet and bag. She didn't seem quite ready for where this conversation was leading. And neither did I.

"I have a meeting with Mr. Pinkerton, Nell," she announced, tying the ribbon beneath her chin. "I'll be back soon. Here are a few pennies for the newspaper."

Chapter 12

In Which Jemma Paints a Picture of Her Last Night

January 12, 1860

Dear Nell,

I like the sound of your name now more than Cornie. And even better, I like writing it with all the ups and downs. Reminds me of a hawk circling and swooping in the sky. It's a real lady's name when I write it out. And I don't mean to sound boastful, but I won the penmanship contest at my schoolhouse here in Saint Catharines.

I am amazed to learn from your recent letter that the Pickled Onion has special powers! That was a good cipher, though it took me a bit to decode it. What does Destiny tell her about you and me? When will I be able to return from Canada?

Please tell me more news of what's happening in America. As much as I love Mama and the babies, I dream each night of going back there. Mama is always scolding me to have more patience. But I want to see where you're living in Chicago and make sure you're not causing trouble! It would be dangerous to return, I know. But I can't stop thinking of the Maple Tree.

Sometimes I want to set off and find him so bad, my feet start to itch.

It used to be that Mama never told me much about the Maple Tree. But now that she knows you're living with the Pickled Onion, well, she's talking some. She's telling me about what happened. And so long as ~~you and me~~ you and I are careful, I'm going to tell you.

The last day I remember in Chemung County was when we were about eight years old and wild as a pair of cottontails. When I think back on it, I probably should have taken notice of what the Maple Tree was doing that day—and my mama, too. They were whispering the whole afternoon and spending time secreted off in the barn. But I didn't pay them no mind.

What I recall most about that last day was swinging off the willow tree into the pond. Do you recollect the same thing? It was like we could fly. I never had a better feeling in my life—as if I was a mighty blue heron spreading my wings.

I didn't know it when I went to sleep that night, but it was the last time I'd ever lay my head down in that old house. Mama woke me up first, it must have been midnight, and said to get my boots. Then she handed me some bags to strap on—they were filled with corn cakes and apples, but I didn't know why. It was pitch-black outside, and she wouldn't tell me ~~nothing~~

anything. (The Pickled Onion's grammar lessons are rubbing off on me.)

Once the babies were wrapped tight in their blankets, I heard the calling of an owl in the front yard. The Maple Tree said that was the signal, and that's when we set out through the woods.

My candle just burned out, so I can hardly see. But I will write one more thing. I was jawing with Mama about the folks at our church. We got to talking about a neighbor of the Maple Tree, and how he lives in a fancy stone house. She said he sure has expensive taste.

"That's Phil O'Dell for ya," she said.

I hope you solve my cipher.

More later.

Your friend forever and ever,
Jemma

Chapter 13

In Which I Get a Promotion

Heck!" fumed Aunt Kitty one brisk March afternoon when I returned from feeding the orange tomcat outside Mrs. Wigginbottom's kitchen. "Heck and tarnation!"

My aunt was sweeping our already spotless floors with such vigor, I thought she would snap her broom. Aunt Kitty had no tolerance for dust and debris to begin with. But when she got worked up about something, she tended to take it out on the rugs, floors, and furniture, and any dirt that might be harbored therein.

"Whatever has gotten into you, Aunt Kitty? I've

never heard you utter oaths like that. Is something wrong?"

She hung her broom on a nearby hook and turned her attention to the drapery. Aunt Kitty had that pickled-onion look again, her mouth puckered up so tight that her lips nearly disappeared.

"Wrong? Well, it most certainly is not right, I can tell you that much!" she said between heavy whacks to the curtains that hung from our frosted windows. "That Mrs. Wigginbottom. Always looking for another dollar. Darn that woman!"

I was so shocked by my aunt's rough language, I had to sit myself down. I chose the rocking chair, not only because it gave me the most comfort to be seated next to the warm fire but also because it was the farthest distance from my aunt and her flailing arm.

"What's she done, Aunt Kitty?" I worried. "Raised the rent again?"

"Worse," she spat. "She's demanding a king's ransom. So pack your bag, Nell. My next case takes me to the state of Pennsylvania, and I will need you to accompany me."

If I hadn't already been seated, I would have

collapsed right across that gleaming floor. Because my knees felt weak when I heard this news.

"What do you mean, Aunt Kitty?" I croaked. My voice was hoarse not only from surprise, but because I could have burst into tears of happiness right then and there. Another chance to join the detectives on a case? I had to fight a smile from spreading across my cheeks.

"That miserly Mrs. Wigginbottom will only watch after you while I am gone if I pay her another ten dollars a week, which I refuse to do. So I have no choice but to drag you along. A boardinghouse is no place for a young girl like you to dwell—especially unattended!"

I had to take a moment and give thanks. Sometimes in life it takes a heaping plateful of Bad to help us appreciate the mouthwatering deliciousness of Good when we finally taste it. And that's how I felt about our dreadful boardinghouse, the wretched meals we were served, and the aggravating theatrics of miserly Mrs. Wigginbottom. If our situation were any better, Aunt Kitty might have left me behind in Chicago.

"Heck and tarnation is right," I said, trying hard to sound like I was sharing Aunt Kitty's frustration. What I really wanted to do was thump her on the back and celebrate. But my aunt was not the kind of person you go around walloping for joy. So instead I knitted my eyebrows in a serious expression and told her, "I'll go fetch my carpetbag, and we can pack."

Aunt Kitty didn't even have the spirit to scold me for my own rough language. She just followed me into the bedroom and started stuffing things into her trunk.

"This could not have come at a worse time, too," she complained. "I just saw an advertisement posted in a shop window about a new home for hopeless children—the Protestant Orphan Asylum, I believe it's called. But I've had no time to pay a visit."

I asked her why she would do such a thing when I was helping her pay the rent like I was.

"Why would I investigate the Protestant asylum? Well, why *wouldn't* I? When the very situation we have before us is a shining example? I have a job to do, Nell. I am a detective! Yet here I am having to bring a sniveling child along with me on my travels!"

I wasn't sure which notion to take more offense to: that she was still looking into orphan homes or that she considered me a sniveler. I chose to ignore her comments and instead kept myself focused on the important matters at hand.

"You should get yourself some more petticoats, Aunt Kitty," I advised her cheerfully as I plunged another one into my bag. "You don't want the newspapers writing that you're a dowdy old matron with no fashion sense. You want them saying, '*The detectives wore petticoats—miles and miles of petticoats.*'"

Aunt Kitty's eyes got squinty, and I knew she was pondering the *s* I had added to *detective*, as if I were now on Mr. Pinkerton's payroll right beside her. But thankfully she didn't make hay about it.

"So you see, Nell," explained Mr. Bangs, the office manager who oversaw all the detectives, "there are not many options that are appropriate for your disguise."

I couldn't take my eyes off the beautiful gowns and tailored men's coats hanging before me. It was later that evening, and I was standing in the back room of Mr. Pinkerton's detective agency, the faint *click-clack* of the horses running up and down Washington Street drifting up to the second floor. There wasn't much worth seeing when you first stepped into the office from the street. Just a heavy wood desk, a few armchairs, and that unblinking eye painted on the glass window.

But once you were admitted upstairs, like I was, since I was practically one of them, well, then you got to see what it meant to be a detective. Mr. Pinkerton's business was like a theater show, with a red velvet curtain draped in a corner to allow folks to change into their disguises. There was one whole room devoted just to clothing and shoes and wigs and false beards.

"Couldn't we take just one little taffeta dress and cut it down to my size?" I asked Mr. Bangs for about the fifth time. I tried to force a dimple, to see if that would finally win him over. But he went on polishing his spectacles and shaking his head.

"That is enough, Nell," came my aunt's voice. I spun on my heels and saw her standing in the doorway. She was trying on her latest disguise—a dowdy gown of dull gray—and her hair was swept back in a severe bun with just a few curls loose at the temples. I felt as if I were gazing into the future: Aunt Kitty looked like a cranky old matron, which was exactly what she was headed for if she didn't start to lighten up.

"Don't make dear Mr. Bangs explain it to you again," she said, with a bit of exasperation coloring her voice. "You've heard the description of the case. You are posing as my companion. You're a modest helpmate, so you do not need a taffeta gown, Nell. Your plain checkered dress will serve just fine."

I stepped away and let the green taffeta fall from my fingertips. I tried to focus on the good news that I was part of Mr. Pinkerton's team of operatives and not on the sad fact that I would have such a pathetic costume.

"Let us go over the details once more," announced Mr. Pinkerton, sweeping into the room with a friendly nod in Aunt Kitty's direction and a hearty slap on the back for Mr. Bangs. Mr. Pinkerton seemed to emerge through a cloud of cigar smoke, his gray eyes beaming. "There's no turning back, Nell. Once you arrive in Philadelphia, you are to assume your new identity wholly. One slipup, and the entire case will be in jeopardy."

I sat right down on the nearest chair, hoping Mr. Pinkerton could not hear me gulp. I had no idea what the word *jeopardy* meant, but it sounded bad. Aunt Kitty stood beside Mr. Bangs, who was holding various hats above her head to determine which worked best with her gray disguise. Her eyes were staring at me hard, and I could tell she was reading my thoughts.

"*Jeopardy* means 'peril' or 'grave danger,' Nell," she said firmly. She didn't even have to remind me that I needed to pay more attention to my vocabulary lists. That was perfectly clear already. "It means this is serious business."

I nodded but still could not find my voice. Mr. Pinkerton sometimes had that effect on me.

"You and Mrs. Warne will arrive in Philadelphia on Thursday aboard the four o'clock train, then proceed by buggy to the nearby village of Jenkintown, which you will call home for the next few days. Mrs. Warne will go by the alias Madam Henrietta Imbert, whose scoundrel of a husband is the noted forger Jules Imbert, now residing in a prison cell. Madam Imbert is devoted to this rapscallion, not only because she loves him but, more importantly, because she loves his money.

"We are targeting a woman by the name of Mrs. Martha Maroney. She will soon be arriving in Jenkintown from the Deep South, where her own husband, Mr. Nathan Maroney, has claimed membership in the brotherhood of scoundrels by—we have clear reason to believe—stealing fifty thousand dollars from the Adams Express Company!"

And when he thundered the amount of stolen money, I nearly fell right out of my chair. That was a sum I'd never uttered once in my entire life. I whispered the number to myself, just to hear my own voice speak a figure so high.

Fifty thousand dollars.

I shivered.

"Nell, we can have you play the part of Miss Charity Englehart. When our suspect's wife, Mrs. Maroney, arrives in Jenkintown, Mrs. Warne is to befriend her, become her confidante, her bosom buddy. You, Nell, are to keep them from being interrupted. The more time Mrs. Maroney spends in the company of your clever aunt, the more likely we will learn what has become of the stolen loot.

"Now, can you handle that, Nell?"

I got to my feet and marched right over to Mr. Pinkerton. And I shook his hand like I was pumping water from a well. Clearing my throat, I told him in the strongest voice I could muster, "It sounds darned good to me, sir."

"Nell Warne, such language," scolded Aunt Kitty.

"Not to worry, Mrs. Warne," said Mr. Bangs with a chuckle. He had settled on a black hat adorned with what looked like crab apples for my aunt to wear. "She has the right spirit, she does. Just give her a few years, and you'll see. Nell Warne will be a great lady someday."

And maybe a great detective, I wanted to add. Or a newspaper reporter. Or a nurse like Florence Nightingale. But instead I just winked at Mr. Bangs to let him know I appreciated the support.

And when he winked right back, I couldn't help but think it was a promise that he would give me a better costume next time.

Chapter 14

In Which Charity Does Not Feel Particularly Charitable

As our train chugged along through Indiana and across Ohio, the sunshine smiling down upon us, I couldn't stop the butterflies from batting around in my stomach. Maybe it was the rattling of the railcar, but I was having a hard time sitting still for such a long journey. I slipped down low in my seat and began reading and rereading Jemma's letters, my eyes lingering on her most recent one. I think she was giving me a cipher to figure out, but how?

"That's Phil O'Dell for ya," I mumbled to myself

as I traced Jemma's words on the page. *"Phil O'Dell for ya."*

"What about Philadelphia?" asked Aunt Kitty, with a vague glance in my direction. She was busy reading an article in the newspaper I'd just finished.

"That's it," I said with a jump, waving Jemma's letter in the air. "Philadelphia must be where the Maple Tree lives!"

Aunt Kitty fixed me with such a look, I knew right away to sit myself back down on my wooden bench and hush. Because the last thing a detective should do is make a complete spectacle of herself. I folded Jemma's letters back into their envelopes and tucked them into my cigar box, but I could not stop my knees from bouncing as we rattled on down the tracks. Jemma's cipher was so good, even Mr. Pinkerton would be impressed.

By the time we reached Philadelphia, I was like a jackrabbit sprung from a snare. Aunt Kitty could barely keep hold of me as we marched through the red-brick train depot and out the doors into the big city. The Maple Tree was out here somewhere, and I would find him.

"Miss Charity Englehart," my aunt snapped, "what has gotten into you? You've never been to this city in your entire life, yet you're walking around as if you know where you're going."

I stopped in my tracks and looked back at Aunt Kitty. She had headed off to the right when we alighted from the train depot, while I had turned to the left.

"I'm just excited to be here," I whispered, dashing back over to her side and skipping to keep up with her fast walking. "I've never been anywhere but the farm and Chicago. This is the most exciting adventure of my life, Aunt Kitty!"

In her tight, clipped voice, she reminded me to call her Madam Imbert. But I thought I saw a smile start to sneak its way up to her eyes. I knew she could appreciate the thrill of adventure. She slowed her fast walking just a bit to let me catch up, and together we admired the redbrick buildings with their cheery white shutters and the bumpy cobblestone roads.

Compared to Chicago, with its muddy streets, muddy yards, and muddy sidewalks, Philadelphia looked tidy. I liked the way the horses' hooves sounded as they trotted down the bright streets. After some time walking, she told me to take note of a special place called Independence Hall, where she said our Founding Fathers and Mothers let freedom ring throughout the land.

I liked the sound of that.

Just as Mr. Pinkerton promised, our buggy was waiting for us across the street, at a restaurant called Mitchell's. After freshening up and taking a bite to eat, we were promptly whisked down the lane to Jenkintown. Our bags were sent up to a room above a tidy tavern, and right away Aunt Kitty and I stepped out for a promenade around town.

To the casual observer, we might have looked like two simple ladies taking in the fresh air. In reality, though, we were keen-eyed investigators, devouring everything in sight: the prim houses, the speeding buggies, the passing faces. With all my senses on high alert, I'd never felt more ready for danger.

And within a few short minutes, we found it. In the form of an angry child.

"I want it now!" wailed the young voice, putting up such a caterwauling, it was enough to make paint peel from the walls. "You're a terrible witch if you don't give it to me now, Mama!"

Aunt Kitty and I rushed to the scene, past a few busy shops and whitewashed fences, until we reached the wide public garden. We were eager to see what the commotion was all about.

"I will do no such thing," answered the child's mother. "It is my peppermint, and I will not share it. Now stop your carrying on, or everyone will think you're a crybaby."

"But I'm not a crybaby!"

And with that, tears flowed and lungs wailed, leaving those of us in the garden to form our own opinions about what did and did not constitute a crybaby. I tugged on Aunt Kitty's arm to slip away before they took any notice of us standing there. But that's the thing about keeping the company of detectives. They're always poking around where any sensible person would flee.

Aunt Kitty stepped right over and introduced herself.

"There, there, darling child," she cooed. "What's the matter?"

Sniffling and wiping at her nose, the girl looked Aunt Kitty over from head to toe and back up again, then sized me up beside her. She did not look impressed.

"I want Mama's candy!"

"Flora Maroney, I already told you," snapped her mother peevishly, moving a round ball of sweets from one side of her cheek to the other. "You cannot have it!"

When I heard that name, my jaw came unhinged, hanging open like a broken dresser drawer. *Maroney?* Could this be our Mrs. Maroney, wife of the suspected robber of the Adams Express Company, Mr. Nathan Maroney?

If so, then the garden crybaby was a Maroney, too.

"May I introduce myself to your darling daughter, ma'am?" I began, turning my charm first on to Mrs. Maroney and then her irritable offspring. "My name is Charity Englehart, and I sure love to play games. Won't you dry your eyes and come along? It would make me ever so happy."

If only those Maroneys knew *how* happy! Now was my chance to show Aunt Kitty and Mr. Pinkerton how helpful I was to have along. My aunt kept her

117

expression calm, but the look in her eyes let me know she heartily approved. And that made me bounce a bit in my boots over my quick thinking. I'd have this child eating out of my hand in no time.

I led little Flora down a stone path toward an open area to play, though her stomping made it clear she was still in the throes of a tantrum. We hadn't walked a dozen paces before she decided to turn her anger on me, commenting about my boots, my bonnet, and finally the size of my ears.

I yanked my hat lower on my head and reached for a sack of sweets I'd tucked in the pocket of my checkered gown. Perhaps a bit of candy might sweeten that sour disposition.

"These boots belonged to my daddy," I said, trying to keep my voice light. "I feel grateful to have them."

"Well, your daddy must not have loved you much to stick you with those unsightly things. And that is the ugliest dress I've ever seen," Flora said, her list of grievances against me growing by the minute. "My mama's gowns are the latest fashions. She has a cage crinoline that makes her skirt flow out like an enormous bell. Your dress is dull and flat."

I decided to hang on to my lemon drops for another time.

"You catch more bees with honey than with vinegar," I advised her tightly, sharing one of Aunt Kitty's bits of wisdom. Then I forced a grin and put my hand out for her to take.

"Bees *make* honey," Flora corrected, stopping in her tracks and letting her scowl hit me full force. "You don't *catch* bees with honey. Any numskull knows that. You could catch a bear with honey, but why in the world would I want to do such a thing?"

And with one swift motion, she kicked me in the shin and raced off down the path toward a cluster of bright yellow forsythia.

Detective work was proving to be more hazardous than it originally seemed.

After about two days' time spent in the company of Flora Maroney, my shins ached from unexpected kicks, my arms were sore from vicious pinches, and my pride was wounded from insults to my general appearance and intellect. But I would never let on to Aunt Kitty. Besides, she was too busy prancing around Jenkintown arm in arm with Mrs. Maroney to take any notice.

"You've done well to befriend darling Flora Maroney," Aunt Kitty told me one night up in our room as I lay on my mattress counting the latest welts from Flora's pinches. "I've confided my tale of woe to her mother, though she has not shared a word about her husband, except to say that he's delayed on business down in Montgomery, Alabama. But she listens closely to my false stories of a jailed husband and how I fend for myself. By taking young Flora away, you're opening the door for her to confide in me."

Aunt Kitty said we would stay another week in Jenkintown and see if Mr. Maroney planned to pay his wife and daughter a visit. And as I pulled the sleeves down on my nightshirt, covering up the marks Flora had given me that day, I tried to remind myself that detective work was much like life itself: every one of us had demons to face down.

Too bad mine happened to take the shape of a fifty-pound tyrant.

When we rose the next morning, Mrs. Maroney was waiting for us in the sitting room of the tavern. Flora was in the yard out front, so I took a deep breath and slipped out the door to keep the child occupied. This would let Aunt Kitty have some quiet time with Mrs. Maroney.

I plunked down on the porch steps and strained my ears, trying to hear their voices through the open windows. But Flora was busy tormenting the tavern's mule, Lucky Pete. It made eavesdropping difficult.

"Mama's going away to see Papa," Flora announced once she'd finally succeeded in getting a rope around Lucky Pete's neck. The poor mule let out such a sad braying, followed each time by a breathless hiccup, it reminded me of Whiskey back in Chemung County. It nearly broke my heart to think of my beloved old mule. But Lucky Pete's wail did nothing to weaken Flora's resolve. She yanked the rope tighter, then tried to drag that animal across the yard.

"I've chosen you to watch over me when Mama leaves town, so long as you give me three candies each day. And you don't get any—that's the bargain. Mama said you don't need no candy, that it would just make your complexion look even worse. So give me your bag. Now!"

I was so dumbfounded by Flora's words, I didn't have enough sense to stop that child from taking my whole sack of lemon drops right out of my pocket.

Watch over her while her mama was gone?

Me?

And what was wrong with my complexion?

Flora tied Lucky Pete to a crab-apple tree, then bounded up the porch steps before I knew what hit me. I looked at the scrawny mule and felt Flora's rope tighten around my neck, too.

"We would be pleased to care for dear Flora in your absence," Aunt Kitty was telling Mrs. Maroney when I came back in from the yard. They beamed over at Flora, who was seated on a small stool by the fireplace now and looking angelic, her dark hair hanging in sweet ringlets. With my lemon drops stuffed in her cheeks, she didn't have the opportunity to sass, so instead she just batted her lashes and nodded politely. "Don't you worry about a thing," Aunt Kitty continued. "Miss Charity will see to all Flora's needs."

Mrs. Maroney wasted no time hightailing it out

of Jenkintown. But Aunt Kitty told me to watch and wait, that Mrs. Maroney was up to something. She had ventured off to Montgomery, Alabama, where her husband was sitting tight—and most likely the stolen money, too. Aunt Kitty felt certain that she was going to come back to Jenkintown with something important in her possession.

"And with you securing her daughter here with us, well, that was a brilliant move," Aunt Kitty said, like we were playing a game of chess and I'd just taken the queen. I didn't bother to tell her that it was Flora calling those shots.

By the time another week passed in the company of Flora Maroney, I had begun to question my desire to participate in Mr. Pinkerton's detective work. I was even pining for Mrs. Wigginbottom's sorry company— anything seemed better than facing another afternoon with our pint-size terror.

"Grab your hat, Charity! One of the operatives just telegraphed that Mrs. Maroney is to arrive today on the two o'clock train," Aunt Kitty whispered at the end of lunch one afternoon as I sat writing a letter to Jemma. I'd just finished half a ham sandwich, the other half surrendered to Flora during one of her tantrums. So I sealed up the envelope and headed for the door. With Flora occupied with the cook's children in the yard, Aunt Kitty and I were free to make our escape.

"We will stroll the street near the train depot and make it appear that we happen upon Mrs. Maroney by chance," Aunt Kitty explained as we took off in a buggy for Philadelphia. The four white horses galloped at a good clip, and Aunt Kitty kept her voice low, so I did not worry that our driver could hear us. But still I leaned in close so I wouldn't miss a single word.

"I suspect she will return from the South with her husband's stolen money—either in her trunk, a bag, or somehow on her person," she continued, her breath smelling of licorice. "I will be watching her every move from the moment she leaves the station, and I ask you to do the same this week as you tend to Flora. If we can catch her with the stolen money, we'll have the evidence needed to solve the case!"

Chapter 15

In Which I Mention Unmentionables

April 22, 1860

Dear Jemma,

    You might not believe where I am right now as I dip my pen to write. So please, if you are wearing a hat, hold on to it. Because I took your note about "Phil O'Dell for ya" to heart, and I am happy to say that is where I am this very moment!

I have looked for the Maple Tree at every turn. But I have not seen him. You say he is a conductor, so I will try to return to the railroad depot and see what I can find. I have met a few porters and ticket sellers, but so far no conductors.

You would not believe the fancy folks who stroll the streets of this fine city. The men are all of them dandies, smoking pipes and wearing colorful cravats at the neck. Their silky black hats are so tall, they remind me of stovepipes. And the ladies appear to have come from Queen Victoria's court. Their gowns are so wide, I have had to clear the path four times already for fear their skirts would knock me off into the shrubbery.

I am always trying to achieve a wider skirt, so I wondered about what I was seeing on the fashionable ladies here. When I peeked in a dressmaker's shop today, I believe I discovered their secret! It was the most unusual contraption, and I can best describe it as a horsehair cage. There are rows of hoops, each wider than the next, that hang from the waist. It flares a gown fuller than even a hundred petticoats. If I had a mind to, I could wear one and have enough room under my flared gown to hang strips of jerky out to dry!

I asked the Pickled Onion if we could inquire about it at the shop, but she would not set foot inside. I insisted we learn more, but she said I should stop bringing up unmentionables.

"Why do you call them unmentionables?" I wanted to know. And do you know what she told me?

"Because true ladies do not mention them!"

I read a sign in the window, and I believe it is called a cage crinoline. Perhaps I will try to make my own when I am not tending to my particular tasks, which I cannot tell you about other than to say my shins are bruised and my arms tender from such dangerous duties as I am performing.

The Pickled Onion has given me ~~permition permissin~~ the OK to mail this letter to you from a hotel here before we return to our tasks. She says you are not to write me back here for any reason. I cannot explain why, so please understand. Just send your posts to the usual address in Chicago, and I will read them when I return.

And since I cannot resist our ciphers, I'll tell you only this: our reason for being here involves LEMONY NOTES. Not ours, of course, but someone else's. I hope you can unscramble that!

More later when I am back home from this adventure. Though I am grateful to be part of it, I was told we'd only be here one week. But it has stretched "interminably."

That is one of my new vocabulary lessons. I believe it means the Pickled Onion owes me a few ginger ales and perhaps a chicken dinner for my suffering.

Very truly your friend,
Nell

Chapter 16

In Which My Keen Eye for Fashion Pays Off

It was on about our fifth stroll past the doorway of the Philadelphia train depot when Mrs. Maroney finally stepped out, accompanied by a porter toting her baggage. We greeted her with exclamations of surprise at the happy coincidence, and she did not appear suspicious to find us there.

"You must be exhausted," Aunt Kitty said with a consoling pat to Mrs. Maroney's shoulder. "Won't you let us take you back to Jenkintown in our buggy? There's room for your trunk and bags. And we could tuck in together in the back and hear all about your trip."

Mrs. Maroney took a slight step backward, away from my aunt's friendly embrace. I noticed she was wearing an expensive-looking new gown with the widest skirt I'd ever seen. It seemed to spread out around her in endless waves of shiny scarlet fabric. She tottered just a bit, momentarily losing her balance, but she refused my help. Aunt Kitty did not seem to notice, as her eyes were on the brown trunk a few steps away, tended to by the porter, and on the colorful carpetbag hanging from Mrs. Maroney's elbow.

"Thank you, Madam Imbert, for your kindness, but I couldn't inconvenience you like that," said Mrs. Maroney, her voice sounding tired. Her face looked worn out, but she was tense and pacing like a turkey before Christmas dinner. "I can hire a buggy on my own and spare you the trouble."

Aunt Kitty's eyes were darting between the trunk and the carpetbag, and I could tell she suspected one of them held Mr. Maroney's stolen loot. Finally she made her move, reaching for Mrs. Maroney's arm and the heavy load hanging on it. In a gesture of kindly helpfulness, she pulled the carpetbag from Mrs. Maroney's clutches. Was the money in that bag?

"You're so good to relieve me of this burden, Madam Imbert. I thought my arm was going to fall right off. Take it, please. I don't know why I thought to pack a dried ham for the journey. I have no appetite."

Aunt Kitty gave me a look, and we both knew the stolen loot was not in that carpetbag. If it were, Mrs. Maroney would have pressed it selfishly to her chest like Flora clinging to my bag of lemon drops. Immediately, we both turned to the trunk.

"Shall I help get this to our buggy, Mrs. Maroney?" I asked, reaching for the wooden handle of the big brown trunk. "Or I could let the two of you ride on together back to Jenkintown, and I'll come later with this here trunk in a hired mule cart."

I beamed at Aunt Kitty, feeling clever at seizing the opportunity to be alone with Mrs. Maroney's plunder. Aunt Kitty even gave me an approving nod, which again made me stand a little taller in my boots. I might not have been doing much detective work playing ghost-in-the-graveyard with Flora this past week. But I could still prove myself useful now and again.

"Oh, I don't care what happens to that old trunk— it's such a bother," came Mrs. Maroney's reply. "Go ahead and ride with it behind us in the mule cart, Miss Charity, and I will fetch it from you tomorrow. I am so worn out, I will take Madam Imbert's kind offer to see me home."

And leaning heavily on my aunt's arm, Mrs. Maroney wandered off toward our comfortable buggy, to ride back to Jenkintown with Aunt Kitty in style. I could hear Aunt Kitty regaling her with tales of "dear Flora," even though Mrs. Maroney hadn't asked. I plopped down on the dusty trunk and watched them walk away, Aunt Kitty in her severe gray gown, Mrs. Maroney in her fashionable scarlet one with wide skirts billowing around her.

Where had Mrs. Maroney hidden that ill-gotten money? If it were in the trunk, she wouldn't let it out of her sight. If it were in the carpetbag, she wouldn't be allowing Aunt Kitty to touch it.

I stared at their two shapes as they made their way down the busy street. And that's when I noticed something. Aunt Kitty was doing her proud walking, like she was balancing the crown of Queen Victoria herself on her head instead of that black hat festooned with crab apples. Beside her, Mrs. Maroney was dragging along as if she had the weight of the world on her shoulders.

Only from where I was sitting, that weight wasn't quite on her shoulders.

It seemed to be more on the midsection. Perhaps, like me, she was wearing layers and layers of petticoats; they certainly could grow heavy through the day. Then suddenly I recalled one of Flora's many insults—this one about my pathetic dress and how droopy it was compared to her mama's gowns. *"She has a cage crinoline that makes her skirt flow out like an enormous bell."*

Mrs. Maroney's crinoline seemed to be weighing her down, and she looked weaker and weaker with every step. She looked, in fact, like something heavy was under that skirt! I took off down the street to catch them, my boots echoing on the sidewalk. But I was too late. They had already climbed into the buggy and were fast away by the time I reached the corner.

I yanked off my bonnet and threw it at the rail post in frustration. I had been so close.

When I bent down to pick up my hat, something on the ground beside it caught my eye. Where

Mrs. Maroney had been standing only moments before was a three-dollar banknote, the words CENTRAL BANK OF ALABAMA printed across the top, a fancy lady cradling a basket of wheat smiling up at me. I gave that fancy lady a grin right back, because this was just the evidence I needed to show Aunt Kitty.

Mrs. Maroney was hiding that stolen money in the cage crinoline under her skirts!

"Well done, Charity!" my aunt whispered during our supper that evening. Always the stickler about staying in character, she had not called me Nell since we left Chicago. "Mrs. Maroney is back at her sister's house across town. We shall pay her a visit tonight and see if we can't find where she's put the money. Perhaps we'll discover a freshly dug hole in the garden or a secret compartment in the corner of the house."

I couldn't wait to snoop around. But I also dreaded having to mind Flora again. I decided to appeal to my aunt's sympathies.

"Aunt Kitty—"

"I am Madam Imbert, and you'd be wise to remember that," she hissed through clenched teeth. It didn't matter that there were no other ears in the dining room with us.

"Sorry," I said, starting over. "Madam Imbert, can't I do something more important to the case than watch that feral child? She'll be the death of me one of these days, the way she's always fussing about how I talk and walk and eat, even laugh. My shins won't last another day with her kicking. Even my daddy's boots can't cushion the blows from her tantrums once she gets going."

Aunt Kitty just blinked, letting my complaints tangle around me like a sticky cobweb. I might not be as annoying as Flora Maroney, but I knew I tested her patience all the same.

"There is always work to be done in this life," she said sternly, her eyes radiating a certain heat that made me uncomfortable. "You can be the hands that lift the load, or you can be the burden itself. You choose."

That was her way of saying she'd heard enough of my whining.

"And speaking of those boots, perhaps it's time

you traded them in for something more appropriate to a young lady," she added, clearing her plate from the table with a little *hmmph*.

"These boots belonged to my daddy," I said, though she was already halfway to the kitchen. "I'll never give them up."

When we stopped round at Mrs. Maroney's that evening, I commenced right away to playing with Flora while Aunt Kitty and Mrs. Maroney sat on the sofa and talked in hushed voices. I knew Aunt Kitty was telling more of her tales of woe about an imprisoned husband, the forger, and Mrs. Maroney was eating it up.

Mrs. Maroney rose now and then, looking tense and tight—though a little lighter on her feet, I observed. She kept pacing back and forth by her cellar door. I noticed Aunt Kitty watching her closely. Then Mrs. Maroney would return to my aunt's side for more stories about a beloved behind bars.

I tried in vain to hear whether Mrs. Maroney was disclosing her secrets about her own wayward husband. But Flora was demanding all my attention, so I could only make out a few words here and there.

Before long, Mrs. Maroney was called upstairs to help her sister fix a broken window. It was going to take Mrs. Maroney a few minutes to tend to the errand, and she excused herself with profound apologies. Aunt Kitty smiled and nodded politely, but the moment Mrs. Maroney disappeared, she raced for the cellar door and was down the stairs in a flash.

"Where's that cranky lady going?" asked Flora, who had just tugged my favorite red ribbon from my hair.

"Madam Imbert? She is borrowing some potatoes," I quickly lied, wondering if that sounded believable. I knew Aunt Kitty was probably poking around down in the cellar in search of the hidden money, but I wasn't about to let on to Flora. "And she is not cranky. She's just firm, that's all."

My explanation seemed to satisfy the child for the moment, which allowed me to step away and gaze up the staircase to make sure Mrs. Maroney wasn't coming back down. My heart was a moth in my chest. What would happen if Mrs. Maroney caught my aunt in the cellar? How would Aunt Kitty explain that one?

The seconds passed like hours, until suddenly I heard footsteps.

Mrs. Maroney was returning from upstairs. But where was my aunt?

"This needlepoint is lovely," I practically hollered as I blocked Mrs. Maroney's way from the staircase into the living room. I was holding up a pillow for both of us to admire, trying to find anything that would cause a few moments' delay.

"Yes, it is beautiful," puffed Aunt Kitty from behind me, her voice a little breathless. She was holding up another pillow from across the room, near the doorway to the cellar. "Your sister has a good eye for detail, Mrs. Maroney."

And it seemed Mrs. Maroney did, too. Because the next thing out of her mouth left us all stunned.

"How did your skirts get muddy, Madam Imbert? Where did you get that dirt? Tell me now!"

Mrs. Maroney was pointing at my aunt, her outstretched finger trembling.

Aunt Kitty must have been on her hands and knees in the dirty cellar, because a big patch of mud was smeared across the lower part of her gown. I saw Flora stand up and crane her neck to glimpse my aunt's skirt, and I swiftly crossed the room to her side.

Flora bounced on her toes, eager to tattle on Aunt Kitty. "She went down to the—"

But before Flora could utter another word, I popped a few ginger candies into her mouth. She looked up at me with shock, but I just waved three more before her eyes, and that was enough to buy her silence.

"I went down in the garden just before we arrived here," answered Aunt Kitty calmly, glancing casually at her muddy skirt. "Tripped and wrenched my ankle pretty badly, but Miss Charity was able to help me along. It's nothing, really."

And with that, Mrs. Maroney was all smiles again and offering to prop up my aunt's foot with one of the pretty embroidered pillows.

"She has made a confession of sorts," Aunt Kitty told me as she sat at the small desk later that night, her lamp casting a yellow glow to our dark room. It was very late, and she was writing a report to send to Mr. Pinkerton in Philadelphia in the morning. She explained bits here and there to me as she wrote.

"What was it?" I asked, rubbing ointment onto my tender scalp where Flora had pulled my hair. "Did she mention the stolen money?"

Aunt Kitty said Mrs. Maroney didn't talk about money. But she did tell Aunt Kitty that her husband was in jail.

"She promises that Mr. Maroney is innocent of all charges," Aunt Kitty said, rolling her eyes to heaven. "But this is the first time she's admitted that her husband is in trouble. She believes he'll be out of jail soon. With no evidence of the crime and no eyewitness, they can't keep him behind bars. He'll be free to spend that loot however he wishes, spoiling little Flora with anything she asks for."

I wanted to say that little Flora was already spoiled rotten. But I decided to spare Aunt Kitty any more of my complaints. Instead I lay my sore head on my pillow and thought long and hard about how to uncover that stolen money.

Chapter 17

In Which I Can Be as Stubborn as a Mule

I t was just a week or so later when Aunt Kitty and I were awoken before dawn by a pounding on our door. I thought the house was on fire, and I was ready to leap from our window or tie our bedsheets into a rope and climb down to safety.

"There's someone downstairs says they need to see you immediately," came the landlord's sleepy voice. "Says it's of the utmost importance. I don't care how important it is, I told 'em nothing comes before a cup of coffee. I'll bring yours to the sitting room."

Aunt Kitty and I quickly dressed and raced down

the stairs. I knew something big was about to happen, so my hopes were high as we reached the sitting-room doorway. But they came crashing down when I laid eyes on Flora perched like a bright bloom beside Mrs. Maroney on the flowery sofa.

"Good morning, dear," Aunt Kitty began in her warm way, embracing Mrs. Maroney with sisterly affection, then patting angelic-looking Flora on her curly head. Nothing flustered my aunt, so she continued in her usual calm voice. "Whatever has you so upset at such an early hour?"

"It's a letter from Mr. Maroney in jail," began Mrs. Maroney, dabbing at her eyes with a lace hankie. "I received it yesterday evening but only read it before bedtime. He's asking me to send him money. Today!"

I gasped, and Aunt Kitty shot me such a look of contempt that even I knew it was time to grab Flora and clear out. We headed for the front yard again, though I made sure to collect my cup of coffee before we passed onto the porch. When it came to minding Flora, I needed whatever strength I could get.

Luckily she was too sleepy to give me much of a hard time. She busied herself with plucking the heads off the bright yellow daisies, and I didn't bother to stop her. Instead I gazed up at the pinkish morning sky and sipped my coffee, listening to the conversation drifting through the open window.

"You can read the letter yourself, Madam Imbert." Mrs. Maroney sniffled. "He wants me to give over everything I have. He says he knows a man who just got out of prison who can help win his freedom. But can we trust him? I've never seen this man! Yet I am to give him everything?"

I could tell by my aunt's silence that she was reading Mr. Maroney's letter.

"What if this correspondence is a fake?" began Aunt Kitty. "Can you judge if it is written in your husband's hand? It could be a forgery."

"It is real," came Mrs. Maroney's agonized reply. Then sheepishly she added, "It is signed with the pet name I call Nathan when we are alone."

I heard my aunt clear her throat. Then in a flat voice devoid of any emotion, she read, *"Your loving husband, Nat-Bat-Cuddly-Wuddly-Cat."*

She cleared her throat again.

"So it is not a fake," wailed Mrs. Maroney. "He

really wants me to hand the money over! Yet I do not want to do it!"

Suddenly I heard another wailing, this time from the yard, and remembered Flora. I dashed down the porch steps and caught up with her, only to find she was back to tormenting the tavern's sweet mule, Lucky Pete.

"You'd best leave this mule alone, Flora," I scolded, raising my voice to be heard over Lucky Pete's piteous braying and hiccupping. "It's not nice to mistreat animals."

She picked up a rock and aimed it at Lucky Pete, who she'd just succeeded in lassoing again with the thick rope. I grabbed her arm just in time and pulled her close to me so I could stare into her eyes. I could tolerate Flora's insults; I could endure her kicks and hair pulling. But I would never, ever abide anyone being cruel to an animal.

Especially not a mule.

"You listen here, you little jackanapes," I began. "You better leave this animal alone, you hear me? You've no right to hurt Lucky Pete, or any other creature."

"My mama says we're rich," Flora answered, fearlessly returning my gaze as if daring me to stop her. "When my daddy comes back, I'm going to get ten mules. Then I'll do whatever I want to them. And you can't stop me."

My enthusiasm for detective work may have been flagging after these long weeks working as this child's nanny. But suddenly it transformed. I made a vow right then and there, before sweet-tempered Lucky Pete and my Heavenly Maker, that I would do everything in my power to stop wicked little Flora Maroney before it was too late.

"Hurry, Charity, into the buggy," Aunt Kitty was hollering a few hours later. "We've got to move fast!"

I leaped into the open buggy and grabbed my seat as the four white horses took off from the tavern, down the lane and out of town. I had to tie my straw bonnet firmly under my chin lest it blow away in the wind as we picked up speed.

"Where are we off to in such a rush, Aunt Kitty?"

"It's Madam Imbert," she whispered, her eyes darting to the driver in the seat before us. "And we're heading to Philadelphia. We need to report to Mr. Pinkerton as quickly as we can, then come right back to Jenkintown. That scoundrel Mr. Maroney is feeling the heat in his jail cell, and he's sending for his stolen money. He plans to have a man come round to collect it from Mrs. Maroney this evening—at six o'clock!"

I wondered if Mr. Pinkerton was going to swoop in and arrest Mrs. Maroney with the money in her hands, or if he was going to follow it all the way back to Mr. Maroney's Alabama jail cell. But Aunt Kitty had other plans, and after we sat down with Mr. Pinkerton at his Philadelphia hotel, I learned what scheming she had in store.

"Here is a copy of the letter from Mr. Maroney," Aunt Kitty explained, setting it on the desk before Mr. Pinkerton in his makeshift office. And trying to keep a grin from her face, she added, "Nathan Maroney's pet name has been verified."

As my aunt and Mr. Pinkerton went over the details of what to do, I studied the letter. It said that Mr. Maroney would send a friend of his, disguised as a book peddler, to call on the sister's house this evening, and that Mrs. Maroney was to give over everything to him. That must mean all the stolen money.

But the word that caught my eye was *trust*.

Mrs. Maroney was to *trust* the book peddler and *trust* her husband, but she already knew that both men had seen the insides of jail cells. Neither could be trusted. While I did not feel a great deal of kindness toward Mrs. Maroney, I did feel a pang of kinship for her situation. Trusting folks was not something I was comfortable with either.

I did not trust that Aunt Kitty was going to let me stay with her forever. Try as I might to believe that she was done thinking about the Home for the Friendless, there were any number of new asylums being built each month in Chicago. Aunt Kitty seemed to value her detective work far above anything else in her life— especially a long-lost, sniveling kin.

And for her part, well, I did not think Aunt Kitty trusted me. When she looked in my face, all she saw was my daddy looking back at her.

"So we have a plan," Mr. Pinkerton was saying, shaking Aunt Kitty's hand with his usual vigorous grip. "We will see you on Shady Oak Lane at three o'clock and not a moment past!"

As Aunt Kitty and I jumped back into the buggy and returned to Jenkintown, I asked her to explain what was ahead.

"Mr. Pinkerton said he would see you at three o'clock, but Mr. Maroney's letter said the book peddler will come at six o'clock. Why the difference?"

"Good ears," Aunt Kitty said, allowing a slight grin to cross her face. "I am glad to hear you're paying attention. I was beginning to have my doubts. Our plan is to send our own book peddler to see Mrs. Maroney. We will take the money hours before Mr. Maroney's man arrives."

I told Aunt Kitty her plan was *sage*, which made her raise an eyebrow in my direction. "It's from my latest vocabulary lesson. It means shrewd or skillful, though you might be confusing it with the herb used for easing sore teeth and gums."

Aunt Kitty kept that eyebrow raised, so I tried to direct us back to the case at hand. "Who will portray the book peddler? I wish Mr. Bangs were nearby to supply the costume."

Aunt Kitty said one of Mr. Pinkerton's operatives was coming down for it—along with Mr. Bangs himself. And I couldn't help but smile, imagining what a thrill it would be for the lucky detective who got to dress up in one of Mr. Bangs's clever disguises and portray the wandering book peddler.

Chapter 18

In Which I Discover a Fondness for Books

Me?"

"We would not ask you if we didn't absolutely need you, Charity," Aunt Kitty was saying.

It was three o'clock, and we were about two miles from Jenkintown, tucked into an abandoned shack in the woods along Shady Oak Lane. We'd come out here to meet Mr. Pinkerton, Mr. Bangs, and the helpful operative who was to portray the wandering book peddler. Only we were missing someone.

"He took ill just before we boarded the train," Mr. Bangs explained.

"But why me? Why do you need me to play the part?" I asked. "How come none of you are doing it?"

"Mrs. Warne cannot for obvious reasons," said Mr. Pinkerton. "And as we've told you, Mr. Maroney described the peddler as having brown eyes. Mr. Bangs has blue eyes, and mine are gray. That leaves only you, Nell."

Aunt Kitty held her tongue, but I knew she wanted to remind Mr. Pinkerton to maintain our aliases and call me Charity.

I looked hard at the three of them standing there waiting for my response. Mr. Bangs was tugging on his thick mustache and watching me with a worried expression.

As much as I wanted to show Aunt Kitty and the others that I could be a good help, I was also a mite bit scared. What if I got caught? Just like Mr. Pinkerton had warned me—and I knew from Aunt Kitty's confounded vocabulary drills—I could put the whole case in *jeopardy*. Mrs. Maroney might see through my disguise, Flora might recognize me by my walk, or any number of things could spoil the secrecy.

"Look deep inside yourself, Nell," whispered

Mr. Bangs with an encouraging wink. "Find the thing that gives you strength."

I took a deep breath and let the air out slowly. Just then a piteous braying rang out from deep in the woods behind us. It was followed by a familiar hiccup, and I knew right away what it was. That sweet mule Lucky Pete must have slipped cruel Flora's rope and run off to celebrate his freedom.

"Yes," I announced with another deep breath. "I will do it. Show me my costume."

Not thirty minutes later, after Aunt Kitty had taken off for town, I began my slow trek toward Mrs. Maroney and her money. My hair was slicked back under a dirty slouch hat, and my dusty boots stuck out from beneath a ratty pair of men's trousers. I wore a threadbare coat that bore grease stains on the arms, and my cheeks were smudged brown with dirt and grime. Mr. Bangs slipped false teeth into my mouth that made my lips curl up as if I were in a permanent sneer, and I hid as much of my face as I could beneath a false brown beard and spectacles. The clothes smelled so bad, my eyes stung with tears, and I knew Mrs. Maroney and Flora would keep their distance.

When I got closer to town, I dragged my left foot with every step, so that if they were watching my approach, they would not recognize me by my gait. *Clomp-drag, clomp-drag.* The only other sound on Shady Oak Lane was the quiet whisper of the wind through the treetops.

"He's here, he's here!" came a wild cry once I reached the fence line of the property. I could see Mrs. Maroney's sister and husband in the doorway. Flora and Mrs. Maroney were standing in the yard staring at me closely. Aunt Kitty was behind them on the garden path, there in her role as the faithful Madam Imbert. She was to offer Mrs. Maroney encouragement to follow her husband's orders in case she wavered.

"Oh, my stars, I cannot bear it!" Mrs. Maroney wailed hysterically, clutching a bulky canvas bag to her chest. "It is too much to ask!"

I tried to ignore her theatrics and focus on my role as the book peddler. Reaching into my bag, I pulled out a neatly bound novel and presented it to her. "Would you like to buy some books?" I said, my words low and husky. My heart was pounding fast for fear that Flora still might know me by my voice. But the false teeth made it so hard to speak, I barely recognized myself.

Mrs. Maroney tilted her head and peered into my face. She was checking to see that my eyes were brown, just as the letter said. Keeping my hands steady, I opened the book and held it up to her. With her own trembling fingers, she took the slip of creamy paper that marked the page. On it was a message written by Mr. Pinkerton just before I'd started down Shady Oak Lane, but it looked enough like Mr. Maroney's handwriting that even I was deceived at first glance.

> My Dearest Wife,
>   This is the book peddler I told you about. Buy a book for Flora. (But only one. You know how she can get.)
>   Give him the entire package for me.
>   Your loving husband,
>   Nat-Bat-Cuddly-Wuddly-Cat

Mrs. Maroney let out a few more anguished wails.

"Madam Imbert, what shall I do?" she cried, her eyes wild. "I want to keep it, but he demands I give it over!"

"You must trust that your husband knows what he's doing," Aunt Kitty said in her calmest voice. "This is part of the plan he has for your happiness. You'll see what adventures lie ahead—for you and for dear, sweet Flora."

Suddenly Flora grabbed at the bag.

"Is there candy in this sack?" she demanded. "Are you giving away my candy? Give it back! Give it back to me now!"

And with that, Mrs. Maroney shoved the canvas bag into my arms and tried to quiet her daughter. As I slowly hobbled my way back down the path and out onto the dusty lane, I could hear Mrs. Maroney calling, "Charity Englehart! Where is Miss Charity? I need her to entertain Flora. Now!"

I tried not to smile, lest my false teeth and beard fall right off my face and reveal my true identity. But my heart was a burning candle of pride, and I could not hide it under a bushel. My *clomp-drag* stride gained a little bounce as I marched back down Shady Oak Lane toward the shack where Mr. Pinkerton and Mr. Bangs waited.

Before long, however, my elation gave way to hard, cold fear. I still had more than a mile of walking ahead of me, carrying what might very well be fifty thousand dollars. I whispered the amount into the wind, again to hear what it sounded like.

Fifty thousand dollars.

I shifted the bulky sack in my arms. With every step, as the woods grew a bit darker, the bag seemed heavier. I jumped at the sound of a twig snapping. I shuddered with every gust of wind. I worried that my luck had turned. What if Mrs. Maroney changed her mind and was chasing me down with a shotgun in her hands? What if she rallied some of the townsfolk to find me, crying, "Robber! Thief! Book peddler!"

Then I heard it. I was about a half mile away from the shack when my ears picked up the rumbling of wheels and the thunder of hooves. A wagon was barreling down Shady Oak Lane from town, and it was going to reach me in a matter of minutes.

I broke out in a run, my daddy's boots carrying me faster than I ever dreamed possible. But the wagon was already on me, and I jumped into a ditch before it could run me down.

"Stand up and dust yourself off this minute!"

That was Aunt Kitty's voice. I popped my head up from the leafy green undergrowth and looked toward the buggy. Four white horses whinnied and stomped, eager to get running again. And my aunt stood at the rail, holding the reins and looking fiery-eyed—like some sort of windblown Messenger of the Apocalypse.

"I said stand up this instant. We've got to hurry! Mrs. Maroney might change her mind, and you're easy prey all alone on this road. Jump in!"

I did just that, and we were off with such a start, my slouch hat flew clean off my head and tumbled down the lane behind us. I decided to peel off my beard, glasses, and stinking jacket, too.

"Good work," Aunt Kitty said with a smile, though she never took her eyes off the road for even a moment. "You were very brave to do that, Nell. And I thank you for your help. Once we collect Mr. Pinkerton and Mr. Bangs, and we head for Philadelphia, we will see what's in the bag. But I believe it is the stolen money. And then we shall know that the honors of the day belong to a girl!"

The pride burning inside me now wasn't just a candle; it was a blazing fire. I looked off to the woods to collect myself. I wasn't used to her making a fuss.

"Thank you, Aunt Kitty," I began, turning back to face her. "You're so brave yourself, I cannot bear to ever let you down."

"What?" she snapped, a little peevish as she urged the horses faster down the lane. "Nell, take those ridiculous false teeth out of your mouth. I can't understand a word you're saying."

I decided the fussing and complimenting could wait for another time.

Chapter 19

In Which Jemma
Explains Cherry Pies
and Railroads

June 29, 1860

Dear Nell,

I know you will not read this until you are
back home in Chicago, but my heart is pounding
to think how close you are to the Maple Tree in
that fine city! I hope somehow you were able to
find him, and that your next letter will be filled
with news about how he is and what he's doing.

It was interesting to hear about the "lemony
notes" in your last letter. At first I thought

you were talking about a "stoney melon," but then I took some more time and figured out what you meant. I sure hope you were able to recover it.

When I told Mama where you were traveling, she dropped a whole platter of biscuits from the shock of it. And that was a real shame, since my sister and brother are like baby birds always chirping to be fed.

Mama's biscuits are as good as ever, but I will tell you that I am catching up to her fast. I hope you do not think I'm proud like a peahen the way I go on about the things I am good at—like my penmanship and running faster than every lazy boy in town. But you should see my pies. They are so pretty to look at, since I can crisscross the crust on top. (It is not hard to do. The secret is to butter your fingers.) And to taste them? Just like Mama's biscuits! You'd fall right onto the floor from the shock of how delicious they are.

Mama doesn't know how much I'm thinking about the Maple Tree and all he's doing. It would hurt her to know I might leave home someday. But I don't have patience for all this waiting around. Why am I up here in Canada when there is so much work to do there? The way I see it, if my cooking is good and my writing is neat, I know I can join in the Maple Tree's work when I find him.

There are folks who help people like us make it to Canada, where we can live free—as free as those blue herons we used to see at the pond together. They are called conductors, and the way they bring us here is called a railroad. Only it's not the kind with wood and spikes that you can see and hear. It's a quiet, secret kind.

That's how me, Mama, and the babies made it to the place we live now, to Saint Catharines. It was through that Underground Railroad. And that's what the Maple Tree is doing today in that fine city you're visiting. He's a conductor for that railroad.

This is not exactly a cipher, but still I hope you can understand my meaning. I am sorry that

I cannot share more. Mama would be angry to know how much I've told you already. And I do not want to write down more in this letter, in case someone reads it who shouldn't be reading it. I don't know what I'd do if I put the Maple Tree in danger.

Mama has company visiting, and they're asking for pie. So I better start slicing. I will write more later.

Your friend forever and ever,
Jemma

Chapter 20

In Which I Take a Shot at Being Aunt Kitty's Teacher

We were back in Chicago by the time Mr. Maroney's trial hit the newspapers. I took comfort in reading that he would remain behind bars and that Flora and her mother would never get their hands on that money again—nor would they ever be rich enough to buy up all the mules she wanted to torture.

Since our return from Jenkintown, I was working harder than ever to stay on Aunt Kitty's good side and avoid the orphan house, the workhouse, or any other living arrangement that meant sending me away. I picked up more of the sewing tasks that Aunt Kitty used to handle. And I was mindful to do a good job with the marketing for Mrs. Wigginbottom—and leave time to barter biscuits for more newspapers and fatten up that orange tomcat on the back porch.

Aunt Kitty stayed on me like fleas on a mangy dog, reminding me all the time about improving my mind so I could better myself. "Do you want to put stitches in holey socks your entire life?" she liked to ask.

I started leaving my copy of the *Chicago Press & Tribune* on the table each day for Aunt Kitty to read, something she was always saying she had no time for. It was my own reminder to her about good habits. She might be drilling me in sums and vocabulary every week, but I made a point to teach her a few things— mostly about the worthiness of reading the daily newspapers and being an Informed Citizen.

Plus a newspaper is just the thing for a snoop like her.

The *Chicago Press & Tribune* was full of stories about fools printing fake money and thieves stealing it, and burglars helping themselves to everything from jewels to liquor to dead bodies in the cemetery. Mr. Pinkerton's detective agency was growing more popular, and his operatives were hailed as heroes for fighting the good fight.

> *Messrs. Pinkerton & Co. deserve great credit...and have won additional laurels by the success which has crowned their efforts. It is dangerous, with such a firm in our midst, to be guilty even of genteel rascality.*

I was standing just outside Mr. Zenger's butcher shop one hot morning, making sure to keep my body in the rectangle of shade his awning was providing, when I overheard some gossip. I knew he was going to drop the price of mutton sooner or later, so I paced here and there as I waited, and I did a bit of eavesdropping.

"I hear that Pinkerton fellow uses voodoo magic to get those criminals to talk," said one old man, shooting a wad of tobacco juice into the street.

"I hear it's whiskey," said another, this one younger and wearing a wilted gardenia in his breast pocket. "He gets them drunk. Then they tell where they've hidden all their stolen jewels. That Pinkerton is a tricky one."

I let out a snorting laugh that even surprised myself. It drew curious looks from the rest of the shoppers. And before I had a moment to gather my wits, I was arguing with the whole lot of them. The old man was spitting and shouting about voodoo trickery, and two women collecting their sausages chimed in with the gardenia man. I was looking to Mr. Zenger for help when suddenly my aunt passed on the sidewalk.

"You come in here and tell 'em, Aunt Kitty," I hollered over the arguing voices, waving my aunt to step into the shade under the wide green awning. "In all the time you've known Mr. Pinkerton, has he ever used voodoo or whiskey to solve a case?"

I was close to snorting with laughter again. Just the thought of such silliness made me grin. But the moment I looked into my aunt's stony face, any trace of the merriment I was feeling vanished like a flock of sparrows.

"I don't know what you're talking about, Nell," she said, her voice so icy, I could have served it with lemonade. "Now I suggest you finish your chores and get on about your business before you find yourself in trouble."

And the way she emphasized the world *trouble*, I could tell I was in plenty.

I raced through the rest of my marketing, rushed into Mrs. Wigginbottom's kitchen with the groceries, and scurried through the cabbage-scented parlor until I caught up with Aunt Kitty.

"They were telling tales about Mr. Pinkerton at that butcher shop," I said stiffly, joining her on the staircase to our room. "I couldn't let them say such things. They called him an abolitionist, too. Said he hides runaway slaves in his own house."

Aunt Kitty was silent, raising a single eyebrow in my direction as her reply. I watched her slip a licorice candy from her silver tin, then snap it shut again.

"What does the word *abolitionist* mean to you, Nell?"

"It means somebody who wants to...abolition something."

I could see that didn't satisfy her. She sucked on her candy and eyed me for a moment or two as we reached the bustling second-floor landing. The neighbor I called Mr. Hummer from the third floor pushed past, and I recognized the song he was humming as "Jeanie with the Light Brown Hair." Then I heard a door bang upstairs, indicating that Mr. Slammer was about.

"Or maybe *abolish* is the word. I hear talk of folks wanting to abolish slavery," I said hesitantly. And when she nodded, I pressed my case. "How can Mr. Pinkerton be an abolitionist if he's from Texas? Everybody knows that's a slave state. Do you think he's really hiding runaway slaves at his own house?"

Once we reached our room, Aunt Kitty shut the door firmly behind her and leaned against it, giving me a long look. Her cheeks were flushed, and it wasn't just from the August heat.

"Do you realize the damage you might have done?" she hissed. "Revealing my identity like that? Silly girl! And just as I'd begun to believe you weren't some foolish child."

I couldn't speak. My face burned with embarrassment. What if someone from the butcher shop, someone who overheard my talk, followed me back to Mrs. Wigginbottom's boardinghouse? Would they know Aunt Kitty was a Pinkerton detective? Would they think that of a woman?

"You are never to discuss Mr. Pinkerton or his

business—or my business, for that matter—with any-one, Nell. Do you understand me?"

I nodded and tried to summon my voice. The voo-doo, the whiskey, the name-calling, I mumbled. They were having a go at Mr. Pinkerton, I explained meekly, and all I wanted to do was set them right.

"You are correct that an abolitionist wants to bring an end to slavery across the land," Aunt Kitty said, her words coming out tight and clipped. "And yes, Mr. Pinkerton is an abolitionist. He is a friend to the slaves and offers refuge in his home here as they journey north to Canada, where they can live free."

Then she paused and finally moved away from the door. Stepping to the fireplace, she began winding the clock on the mantel. "But you are wrong about his country of origin. Mr. Pinkerton hails from Scotland, not the Wild West."

Scotland or Texas, they both sounded foreign to my ears.

"I'm sorry, Aunt Kitty," I began. But I didn't know where else to go with my apology. "I just—"

"That's enough, the damage is done," my aunt said, heading for the back room and rummaging around in the big, wooden wardrobe. I saw her fumbling with a pale yellow hatbox, then slipping a silver object into her bag.

"I believe you can make amends," she said, her skirts swishing as she crossed the room again and reached for the door. "Now grab your sunbonnet, and we'll go.

"And stop calling me Kitty."

We were back in the blinding sunshine in moments, and I raced after her until we reached State Street. We climbed aboard the clattering omnibus just as it pulled up, and it carried us all the way to the southern edge of the city, where the prairie grasses grew tall and abundant. The summer heat was drying out the land, and beyond us stretched empty fields turning from green to golden. Since I was finished with my obligations to Mrs. Wigginbottom, I figured Aunt Kitty wanted us to take a leisurely stroll along the lakeshore back to the city.

"Are you and me out for a meander, Aunt Kitty?"

"You and *I*, Nell," she corrected, straightening her bonnet as we stepped away from our ride. "Do you never study your grammar lessons? And no, we are not out for a *meander*, though I do recognize that from last week's vocabulary drill."

Once the omnibus was out of sight and we could no longer hear the horse's hooves, she handed me something heavy and cold. "I have observed the scar on your hand, Nell. It tells me you can shoot. But what I want to know is, Can you shoot well? Well enough to teach me?"

You could bet a stack of rabbit skins I was a decent shot! An empty stomach made a good teacher. And as much as I loved holding a cottontail in my arms and rubbing its soft fur with my cheek, I loved it even more in a stew with a few carrots.

I took hold of my aunt's silver weapon and turned it around in my hands. I squeezed one eye shut and pointed it off toward a cluster of trees and the lake beyond.

"Just so you understand what you're dealing with, Aunt," I began, "a gun like this here revolver made by Mr. Samuel Colt is a killing machine, plain and simple. And as you see from my scar, you can hurt your own self as much as what you're—"

BANG!

We stared off toward the pale gray rocks in the distance, where a bit of dust kicked up from the bullet.

"—as much as what you're shooting at. And frankly," I added, "if you're not careful, it can knock you flat on your fanny."

She thanked me for my warning, though her voice lacked conviction. I was pleased, however, that she wanted to know more. Pushing the gun back into my hands, my aunt asked how she was supposed to shoot it.

"You have to show me, Nell."

"Why do you need to learn to handle a gun, Aunt Kitty? Is your detective work getting more dangerous?"

Silence was her only reply. And that told me enough. She wasn't investigating the jewelry heists and grave robbing I'd read about in the newspapers. For Aunt Kitty, the stakes were getting higher. And that I'd just compromised her identity this morning at the butcher shop—well, I felt a knot tighten in my stomach.

I shuddered to think of my aunt pulling a gun on a criminal. Would that criminal point one right back at her? I knew guns were for taking lives, but in my mind, that was limited to small critters we needed to eat. What would it be like to squeeze the trigger on a man? Or woman?

Once a bullet was fired, there was no calling it back.

I looked off at the lake, as blue as the late-summer sky, and I let some thoughts wrestle with each other in my mind. On one hand, "Thou shalt not kill" was about as crystal clear a sentence as had ever been written. But on the other, I did not want to attend Aunt Kitty's funeral.

Finally I determined that I was a crack shot, and she'd be hard pressed to find herself a better teacher than me. So I vowed to show her everything I knew.

I raised the gun and again pointed it toward the lake. My arms were warm from the sun, but my fingers remained cool and nimble. I aimed for a broken branch that was dangling from a tree about fifty paces away. Again, the *BANG!* that emitted from the revolver made Aunt Kitty jump. She grabbed at the straw bonnet on her head, leaping back as the branch exploded in the air and rained down on the ground below it.

"You can take six shots before having to reload,"

I explained, trying again to place the smoking gun in her hands. But she pushed it back to me and waved her long, gloved fingers toward the trees.

"But what do I do to make it shoot, Nell? How do I *use* it?"

I took aim at another tree and slowly walked her through the steps.

"You get your prey in sight," I whispered, her breathing fast behind me, "pull back the hammer"— her breath caught—"then gently squeeze the trigger."

BANG!

This time she was ready for the shot but not the quarry. We both gazed up at the tree where I'd fired and stood there in wide-eyed wonder as a squirrel fell right out, deader than a slab of bacon.

"Thank you, Nell," Aunt Kitty said cheerfully, finally taking the warm revolver from my hand. "This demonstration has proven quite useful. We even have something to bring back to Mrs. Wigginbottom's kitchen."

Chapter 21

In Which I Tell Jemma About My Fretting

August 22, 1860

Dear Jemma,

    I did not know those secrets about the railroads, and I imagine how much you worry about the Maple Tree. He is a brave soul, as are all of those who travel on it. Now I understand why you want so badly to come back and help folks. You would be good at it. But I believe every hair on my head would fall out from all the worrying I'd do over you. It would be dangerous work, that's for sure.

Things here in Chicago are ~~muggy~~ ~~full of holey socks~~ fine. We ate squirrel tonight, and it reminded me of the days when ~~you and me~~ you and I went hunting with slingshots, back when we were young ones. You always had good aim. Do you still? Maybe it's another one of your many talents to add to pie baking, fancy writing, and beating boys at footraces. You never know when it might come in handy.

I still have pretty good aim as well, though firing off my mouth is another thing entirely. I am working harder than ever to keep myself helpful to the Pickled Onion. I'm always worried she's going to come home one afternoon and tell me she's done it, that she's made arrangements for me at some wretched orphan asylum. So I make sure she hears my coins clink into the money tin on her shelf.

When I get to complaining about the Pickled Onion, I remind myself how hard country life was. And then I feel grateful to be here with her in Chicago, even if I do have to stay one step ahead of the orphan house.

The other day, when the Pickled Onion was pestering me about my grammar and vocabulary and bettering myself, she asked me what I aspired to in this life. I did not admit my interest in following in her footsteps, though I do find her line of business exciting. I told her about my newspaper dreams, as well as my admiration for Miss Florence Nightingale and her fame as a nurse.

Do you know what she asked me in reply?

"Why would you dream of being a nurse and not a physician?"

Can you believe such a thing? She declares that any woman can do the same things a man can do. And that means performing a man's job, too, like she's done.

I shouldn't let on too much, but I'll tell you this little cipher. The Pickled Onion seems to take a Colt along with her now, but not the kind that needs a saddle.

Our landlady is shouting for me, so I have to run. But one last question. Have you heard folks talking about Mr. Abraham Lincoln there? He's trying to stamp out slavery from the land. Maybe if he does, you can come back from Canada safe and sound. Then you and I will sit down over cups of hot coffee and slices of cherry pie, and we will savor every last one of our secrets together.

Very truly your friend,
Nell

Chapter 22

In Which Aunt Kitty Transforms into a Southern Belle, and I Get a Bit Choked Up

utumn arrived a few weeks later, and I kept myself busy with as many jobs as possible. I kept my mouth shut, too. I was marketing after noontime each day for Mrs. Wigginbottom and becoming known for my shrewd bargaining. And I was darning so many holey socks at the boardinghouse, my nose had grown numb from the particularly brutal odor of sweaty, dusty feet. I even picked up odd jobs over at Mr. Pinkerton's detective agency, sewing stylish trousers and cotton shirts for Mr. Bangs and his costume supply.

I was happy to do whatever I could to stay in Aunt Kitty's good graces. Her observations about orphans and more homes for the friendless—"I just saw an advertisement for another new asylum, this one opened by the Catholics!"—still made my ears prick up like a nervous deer's. But I tried to keep one step ahead of my aunt's intentions.

"You made it clear from your time with Flora Maroney that you can play ghost-in-the-graveyard," Aunt Kitty announced one crisp afternoon. "But can you haunt?"

I was busy with my petticoat project. While I could not find the right materials to build my own cage crinoline, I still wanted a wide skirt—wide enough to hide a flock of chickens under it if I liked. So with my head bent and my mind focused on my stitches, her query took me by surprise.

"Graveyards, ghosts," I said, after a moment to collect my thoughts. "They both can get a body shaken up. But I ain't—er, *haven't*—ever been frightened by either yet. Why do you ask?"

"Mr. Pinkerton was impressed by what he calls your 'mastery of disguise' in both the fortune-teller case and the Maroney adventure," Aunt Kitty said, her hand slowly running a dustrag over the long fireplace mantel. "He asked me if you might be spared from your duties here at the boardinghouse to perhaps take part in another investigation."

I jumped to my feet, letting my sewing drop to the floor in a cloudy white heap.

"You bet I can be spared!" I answered, nearly hollering. "There's nothing I'm doing here with Mrs. Wigginbottom that can't be taken up by one or two of those shifty bachelors like Mr. Slammer or Mr. Hummer for a few days. I'd be more than willing to chase down scoundrels and bring criminals to justice."

"Well, I told Mr. Pinkerton no, of course," Aunt Kitty said, finally turning from the fireplace and facing me. "A girl of your age participating in detective work? It's outrageous. The danger, the risk to life and limb—"

"You don't have to worry about me, Aunt Kitty," I protested.

"I am not worried about you, Nell. I'm worried about the rest of us! I'm worried about the danger we operatives would face if you should slip up again and reveal our charade!"

I tried to catch my breath. How could she tell Mr. Pinkerton no? Here was another chance to prove myself, to show Aunt Kitty that I was made of good stuff—despite what she thought about my daddy. And I wanted to prove myself to Mr. Pinkerton, too, so he'd see that I could turn into a great detective someday. But she'd snatched it away.

I could have spit, I was so angry.

"However, Mr. Pinkerton can be a force of nature when he gets an idea in his head," Aunt Kitty continued with a sigh. She walked over toward the peg where her straw broom was hanging. "He will not drop the idea of your joining our entourage for this next case. While he intends to hire more women for the detective force, he has not yet had the chance. So you, Nell Warne, have been requested to report for duty at five o'clock today at Mr. Pinkerton's office. Do you accept?"

I didn't even bother to pick up my half-mended petticoat from the floor. I grabbed my bonnet and wrap, whipped open the door, and left Aunt Kitty behind. She could yammer on with the dust mites until suppertime for all I cared. I had important business to attend to.

"What are you doing with those feathers?" I asked the next morning as our train rolled south across the wide, flat prairie toward Mississippi. I was watching Aunt Kitty stitch brown and blue pheasant feathers to an otherwise respectable black-velvet bonnet. I recognized those feathers to be the very ones that came off the bonnet she'd found on our landlady's stoop a few months ago. I'd have to tell Jemma more about Aunt Kitty and her frugality.

"I'm creating part of my costume," she said in a low voice. There were only a few other riders in our railcar, but I knew how important it was to remain undercover. I peered around at our fellow passengers, studying their faces one at a time. Was there an eavesdropper right here among us? A criminal?

"Could we talk more about the case we're on?" I whispered, scooching closer on the wooden bench across from her. "Mr. Pinkerton talked so fast yesterday evening. I'd feel better knowing a few more of the particulars."

Aunt Kitty nodded in agreement, though her eyes

stayed fixed on her sewing. She took her time explaining the heart of the matter as she slipped her everyday bonnet from her head and substituted the flouncy, feathery one in its place. The long pheasant feathers made it appear that a large bird had nested and died up there.

"Here are the facts as I understand them," she began quietly. "A bank teller was murdered in cold blood, and money was stolen. Even more money, in fact, than the fifty thousand dollars in the Maroney case. The sum stolen in this bank murder was one hundred and thirty thousand."

I stared out the window at the scenery rushing past, trying to imagine all those zeroes. Aunt Kitty said the bank's president asked Mr. Pinkerton for help solving the crime and getting that money back. And the lead suspect was a man of high society: the dead bank teller's best pal.

I couldn't help but gasp. A best friend like Jemma?

"And as Mr. Pinkerton explained, our job is to befriend the suspect and other townsfolk. Until we've solved this case, you and I shall go by the alias Potter. I will be known as Mrs. R. C. Potter, and you, Nell, will portray my niece Penelope Potter. We will be staying at a local hotel in Atkinson under the pretense of my being of ill health and in need of rest and recuperation in beautiful northern Mississippi. You will be accompanying me to help me convalesce."

I stared at her blankly for a moment or two, turning that word around in my head.

"*Convalesce* means 'to get better,'" Aunt Kitty said testily. "And we will drill vocabulary along with sums nightly during our Southern sojourn."

I smiled and bounced heartily on the railcar bench, fluffing up my washed-out, red-checkered dress. I didn't care how many vocabulary words she was going to make me memorize. This sure beat the pants off marketing for day-old meats. And Mr. Pinkerton had mentioned something about my playing a ghost this time, which sounded much easier than playing with an unruly child.

Before long the door opened on the railcar and Detective Webster appeared. Since I'd been helping out stitching the detectives' costumes, I'd become friendly with a few of the agents, and Mr. Webster was the merriest. Like a playful uncle, he was always ready to tease.

"Good afternoon, ladies," he said, with a formal bow and tip of his hat. And taking a seat next to Aunt Kitty, he gave my arm an affectionate punch.

I couldn't resist the urge to punch him right back, which made him utter a howl that quickly transformed into a belly laugh.

"Nell Warne," he said in a low voice so he wasn't overheard, "your aunt tells me all sorts of things about you. But she's failed to mention your right hook. You've got quite an arm, for a girl."

"She's got quite an arm—period," Aunt Kitty corrected with a smile. "She's as strong as any boy, Mr. Webster, and you'd be wise to remember that!"

"Oh, I know never to underestimate the ladies, Mrs. Warne," he declared. "Women are like coffee—strong and bracing, but if you're not careful, they'll make you jumpy and irritable. Consider me 'Warned.'" And he laughed hard at his own joke, which set Aunt Kitty laughing, too.

She gathered her things to join him for a meeting

in the next car with Mr. Pinkerton. But before she left, Aunt Kitty leaned in close and whispered, her breath smelling faintly of licorice.

"We'll be making a rest stop soon, and I want you to use that time to change into your disguise from Mr. Bangs. You'll find it in my green carpetbag. And I believe there are enough pheasant feathers to make a fashionable new bonnet for you, too. We are Potters now, Penelope. When we arrive in Atkinson, we should be in full costume."

And with a quick nod, she was gone.

I decided I would show Aunt Kitty my *Godey's Lady's Book* magazine when she returned, so she could see the latest fashion in bonnets. I did not want to parade around Mississippi wearing one of her deceased, winged friends on my head.

Heaving her overstuffed carpetbag up onto the bench across from me, I undid the clasp. Reaching in, past a pile of apples and a wrapped loaf of Mrs. Wigginbottom's Indian cornbread, I felt around until I touched the soft material of what must have been a gown of some sort. With two hands I unfurled it, only to behold the most beautiful, most fashionable, most exquisite dress I had ever laid eyes on. Frills of flowery orange silk tumbled to the floor, the glossy fabric whispering about me.

My cup of happiness didn't just runneth over right then. It was spilling all over that railcar and making a complete mess of things.

"I got something in my eye," I said to the empty seat across from me, quickly turning my face to the window. I wiped my nose on the sleeve of my sad checkered dress and took a deep breath, trying mightily to get ahold of myself.

But I couldn't.

Nobody had ever given me such a thing of beauty in my whole life. Just the thought of getting to wear something so lovely sent me bawling like a bald-headed baby. Who needed a fashion book like *Godey's* when she had a dress like this one to wear?

We hadn't been in town for even half a day before we were introduced to the high society of Atkinson, Mississippi. Aunt Kitty, or I should say Mrs. Potter, was a sight in her sizable bonnet with the bird roosting atop. But her red-and-gold-plaid gown with full petticoats, which I recognized she'd sewn from her fortune-teller costume, was the envy of all.

"Mrs. Potter, it's a pleasure to meet you and Miss Penelope," the Atkinson ladies were saying, with formal bows and curtsies. There was so much bobbing and grinning and nodding up and down, they looked like a covey of quails. Their eyes devoured Aunt Kitty's dress, taking in all the flounces, as well as my gorgeous one with its bell sleeves and tiered skirt. But when their gazes landed on one of my scuffed brown boots peeking out from beneath the hem, the fussing over us stopped, and Aunt Kitty felt the need to fill the awkward silence.

"My niece Penelope has an affliction of the foot," she said, shooting me a look that could have set fire to kindling wood. "Her boots ensure, *ahhh*, that her bones grow straight."

I smiled and nodded, feeling more magnificent than one of their Mississippi magnolia blossoms. And frankly, my daddy's boots had never looked better, draped by the beautiful floral skirt as they were.

"You must dine with us tonight," insisted one of the society ladies. Her name was Mrs. Drysdale, and she had gentle eyes that drooped down just a hint at each corner, giving her a sweet, doelike appearance. "Both you and Miss Penelope."

Aunt Kitty was eager to take her up on this offer and get some clues to the murder mystery, so we called at Mrs. Drysdale's home at six o'clock sharp. The other society belles were already there, and they made quite a fuss over us again as we entered the grand foyer.

"Please, won't you follow me into the dining room," Mrs. Drysdale was saying with another few curtsies. Aunt Kitty and I did our fair share of gracious dipping and bowing and bobbing, then we tromped off toward the table. Only I guess I might have been the only tromper, because Aunt Kitty gave me another severe look.

When we stepped into the dining room, the other guests drifted around the long table and began taking their seats. But I noticed a well-dressed man in the far corner of the room standing as still and stiff as a candlestick. He was gazing out the window, seeming unaware that the room behind him had filled up.

"Mrs. Potter, I'd like to introduce you to my husband, Mr. Drysdale. He's a bit distracted lately, as his dear friend was recently taken from this world in a terrible, violent manner."

Mr. Drysdale turned from the window at the sound of his name and seemed to snap back into the present moment.

"Pleasure to meet you, Mrs. Potter," he said, bowing his pale face toward my aunt and forcing a smile. His expression looked nervous, and there were dark circles under his eyes. "And your niece Penelope Potter, I presume? Mrs. Drysdale told me of your arrival."

When he turned to me, a chill raced so quickly across my back and shoulders, I actually looked beside me to see if a mouse had scurried out the bottom of my petticoats.

"Let's all take our seats, shall we?" directed Mr. Drysdale with a vague wave of his arms. He turned to a white-haired lady on his right and launched immediately into a dull conversation about the weather, and soon the whole table was buzzing with the usual pleasantries.

"Is that our suspect?" I whispered to Aunt Kitty as I fumbled with my napkin.

"According to Mr. Pinkerton," she said softly, a smile painted on her lips as she realigned her fork and knife, "Mr. Drysdale is the one, yes."

"He looks weak as a sickly lamb," I observed, folding and refolding my napkin and pretending to be absorbed in my place setting. "How do you suppose he committed the murder?"

Aunt Kitty turned to her left and greeted the elderly gentleman seated beside her, the ancient husband of one of the other society mavens.

Turning back to me, she whispered, "A hammer." Then, passing me a platter of dinner rolls, she added, "Three blows to the head."

I coughed so hard that one of the servants had to escort me from the room to sit in the foyer with a glass of mint tea until I got ahold of myself.

Chapter 23

In Which I Tell Jemma
of the Deliciousness of Our
Latest Escapade

September 19, 1860

Dear Jemma,

Exciting news! My last letter was
written in Chicago, but now I am gazing
out upon a lush green countryside and
writing to you from a porch swing, which
might explain my wobbly handwriting.
(Though you already know how bad my
penmanship is compared with yours.)
The Pickled Onion's work brought us

to another exciting city just a few days ago.

I don't dare reveal which of the glorious thirty-three states in the Union we're visiting this time, lest she spy on my letter and throttle me for sharing secrets. Do you recall our old neighbor, the one who was always borrowing my mule, Whiskey, to help her move stones in her yard? I believe her name was Olive Ippy. Well, we're down where Mrs. Ippy lives now, if you catch my meaning.

The Pickled Onion ~~and me~~ and I have settled into a beautiful hotel that has the softest bed I've ever slept in. You won't believe how fluffy the pillows are here. And the sheets are so silky, I slip right onto the floor every time I roll over.

The food is like tasting heaven. After all those sorry meals at the boardinghouse, I thought my tongue had withered up and died. But just like Lazarus, my mouth has come back from the dead.

For mealtime, we choose what we want off a menu that is written in penmanship as pretty as yours. Today at supper, I wanted to pick one of everything they were offering—boiled, broiled, roasted, pickled. They had things from water and from land, hot and cold, stuffed or not. My favorite was a dish that came all the way from the country of Italy—they called it Macaroni a l'Italienne with Fromage de Parmesan. How's that for fancy eating? And to finish me off, I sunk my teeth into two slices of pecan pie.

I was so full, the Pickled Onion nearly had to roll me back to our room.

Tagging along with her ~~ain't~~ ~~aren't~~ isn't so bad. I don't know how I'll ever go back to boardinghouse living after this.

Very truly your friend,
Nell

Chapter 24

In Which Aunt Kitty Takes a Fall, and I Rise to My Vocabulary Lessons

How did we come to own such beautiful gowns? I didn't see you stitching this orange one at the boardinghouse."

Aunt Kitty was brushing dust off her sleeves as we let our horses walk along the lane outside Atkinson. It was a sunny day just a week or so after our arrival. "Mr. Bangs made yours," she explained. "He asked me about your favorite color weeks ago. And as you noticed, I sewed mine myself."

I imagined sweet Mr. Bangs tending to things back

in Chicago. While Mr. Pinkerton was steel-eyed and sharp, Mr. Bangs was like butter.

"We should visit a photography studio while we're here," I said eagerly. "For the sake of Mr. Bangs. Don't you think he'd be happy to see how good we look in our costumes, Aunt Kitty?"

"Mind yourself, Penelope," she snapped.

I rolled my eyes. Must she always be a stickler for staying in character? The only living souls to overhear us on this back road were our horses and perhaps the occasional hoot owl.

"A photograph is an extravagance. We've no need for it."

"Don't be so old-fashioned, Aunt," I pushed. "Wouldn't you love to have an image to put in a frame—something to be remembered by?"

"I sat for a camera once in my life. My Matthew carried the image with him everywhere, so we'd never be apart. I believe it was still in his pocket the day he died. I never saw it again."

There was no sadness in her voice, just the flatness that honesty sometimes demands. I wanted to trot after her and ask whatever happened to the picture, but I didn't dare. Aunt Kitty was too private for that.

I urged my horse on and caught up with her, tasting a little grit in my teeth from the dusty road.

"So how are we going to crack this case?" I asked, eager to start a new subject.

Aunt Kitty said she was asking herself the same thing.

"That sly Detective Webster has befriended Mr. Drysdale," she said. "But we've got to get closer. We've got to gain Mrs. Drysdale's trust."

"We should visit for tea or call on her for another dinner party," I plotted.

"No, even closer somehow. We've got to see the Drysdales' comings and goings. We've got to try to get inside Mr. Drysdale's head."

I suggested we camp out in the woods behind the Drysdale house, though it was with some hesitation. I was fond of those silky sheets back at the hotel, not to mention the fancy food. I wasn't sure I could leave them for a bedroll in the woods and squirrel for supper. "That's about as close as we can get to those Drysdales."

Aunt Kitty studied her licorice tin, opening it slowly and popping a candy into her mouth. And for the first time since I'd come to live with her, she held the tin open to me and offered to share. I popped a piece right into my mouth, too surprised to utter a thank-you.

It was dreadful. The bitterness was so sharp, I might as well have been sucking on a lump of coal. I felt my eyes water and knew with certainty that my teeth would be black for an hour.

Licorice was just another thing that my aunt and I would never see eye to eye on.

"If this is anything like the case with Flora and Mrs. Maroney," I began, moving my tongue around in my mouth and trying to clear the licorice taste away, "we're going to need evidence. Or perhaps an eyewitness."

"Or both," Aunt Kitty said softly, as if her mind were a hundred miles away. "Unless the killer himself confesses."

After a few minutes, she closed the licorice tin with a snap that made our horses' ears twitch. And she announced she had a plan that would get us as close to the Drysdales as possible. I was to go along with her no matter what might present itself. Aunt Kitty asked me to trust her and ask no questions. I wasn't confident I could do either.

Trust her? When the thought of her sending me off to an orphanage still gnawed at my mind? And ask no questions?

Now, how was I supposed to do that?

"It's time we head into town," she said with glance at a nearby tree. I could tell she was measuring up its shadow to determine the approximate hour. But I didn't need a short shadow to tell me it was lunchtime—my stomach's growls were making it pretty clear. "We're to meet the ladies for a ride, Penelope."

She took off cantering back toward the center of town, where the society belles were gathering for an afternoon outing. I trotted along behind her, eager to get a glimpse of a picnic basket that promised fried chicken and buttered biscuits. But unfortunately I saw no such thing.

Before long we joined the party of frilly-dressed

matrons and a few white-haired gentlemen as they climbed into their saddles.

"Are the boots uncomfortable in the heat, Miss Penelope?" one of them was asking me, her forehead crinkled up like a dumpling as she tried to appear sympathetic. "An affliction of the foot must be hard on a young girl."

"They're remarkably comfortable, ma'am," I asserted, trying not to take offense at her clear disdain for my favored footwear. I forced a grin and let my mare trot on ahead.

We kicked up a storm of dust as we galloped along another lane into the country. I was deep in thought—my mind like the pendulum on a grandfather clock, swinging back and forth between vivid thoughts of a fried-chicken lunch and the holey head of the hammered bank teller—when a scream yanked me back to the here and now. I looked up and saw Aunt Kitty racing ahead of the rest of us, her horse bolting out of control like it had been bitten by a snake.

"Aunt," I shouted, mindful that I'd best not revert to calling her Aunt Kitty and reveal her true identity. "Aunt, come back!"

By the time the rest of us caught up with Aunt Kitty, she was lying in the road looking limp as a rag doll. My heart was in my throat as I hurled myself off my mount and raced to her side. I'd seen enough of my family pass from this world—I couldn't bear another loss.

"Are you all right, Aunt?" I gasped, pulling her head into my lap and brushing the dirt from her hair. My hands were trembling as they touched her face. Her cheeks were hot and a deep pink.

"Let Mrs. Drysdale do this," she hissed through clenched teeth, opening one fierce eye to stare up at me. "Make room for her."

Immediately I knew Aunt Kitty was fine and this was part of her scheme. I fought the urge to throw my arms around her neck and hug her for joy. Instead I scooched aside as Mrs. Drysdale rushed to help.

"Good heavens, Mrs. Potter!" she said urgently, clumsily adjusting my aunt's head and placing it on her full skirts. "You're alive! I thought for sure that horse had broken your neck."

My aunt mumbled something indecipherable and made her eyelids flutter groggily. The effect was convincing, and Mrs. Drysdale called to the others for help.

"We just happen to be in front of my property," she announced. "We'll take Mrs. Potter into my home to recover. By the looks of it, she'll need plenty of bed rest before she'll be herself again."

And that was how we moved into the bedroom next door to a murder suspect.

"I will sleep with the fireplace poker in my hands," I was telling Aunt Kitty as I plopped down on the lumpy feather bed, the heavy iron bar across my lap. "If I hear anything out of the ordinary tonight, I will start swinging. And as for you," I added, my eyes on her yellow hatbox, "I assume you brought your Colt. One cannot be too cautious when sleeping so close to a homicidal hammerer."

Aunt Kitty sighed and lifted that eyebrow of hers. She was not one to tolerate theatrics. But this was no comedy playing out upstairs at the Drysdale house. We were residing just ten paces from someone who was quite possibly a villain of the foulest kind. We had to be alert, aware of our surroundings, and above all else, armed! But try as I might to convince my aunt of this, she seemed to think I was being dramatic.

"Surely by now you know that your strongest weapon is right here," she said, tapping her temple. "Besides, there are two of us and one of him, Penelope," she added, tugging a hairpin from her bun. "I believe you can do that arithmetic."

She could dismiss my preparations if she wanted, but I likened our arrangement to the night I had to fight off a pushy raccoon back on the farm. Whiskey was at my side, but that raccoon didn't give a hoot about being outnumbered. The only thing to make him hightail it out of our barn was the sound of my pitchfork *whooshing* past his ear.

"Sometimes a girl has to take a stand," I explained in a serious whisper. "And while I'm all for using my smarts, I feel a good bit more comfortable knowing I've got something to back it up. Preferably made of iron."

Suddenly, a bump in the room next door made us both freeze. It was Mr. Drysdale moving about. Was he planning to pay us a visit? I clutched the fireplace poker and raised it to my shoulder. Aunt Kitty gestured for me to sit down, but I wasn't about to pay her any mind. We stood there in the yellow light of the single oil lamp, our ears listening for even the faintest noise.

In my mind's eye, I tried to imagine Mr. Drysdale and his friend, the hammered bank teller, in better days. I pictured them laughing over a joke or sitting down to enjoy a root beer. They were best friends, just like me and Jemma. What kind of person would bring harm to his best friend, I mumbled to myself. Was it really possible Mr. Drysdale would do such a thing?

"It's not only possible but probable," whispered Aunt Kitty, giving the belt on her robe a quick tug.

"But why?" I asked, using the iron poker to scratch an itch in the middle of my back.

Aunt Kitty said the signs all pointed to the money—one hundred thirty thousand dollars was a grand sum. "And that's another lesson for you, Penelope."

"What lesson?" I whispered. "One head plus three hammer blows equals...?"

"Don't sass me. It's a lesson about the evils of money."

A sound in the garden down below caught my attention, and I dashed over to the open window. A figure was moving across the yard, the white of its nightshirt catching the moonlight.

"It's him," I whispered, calling Aunt Kitty near. "That's Mr. Drysdale out there in the yard. Where is his robe, for decency's sake? And what's he doing?"

"I'll get my slippers. You stay here and keep watch."

Now, lots of thoughts scattered around my head just then, spilling here and there like marbles from a bag: it was well past midnight. We'd come all the way to Mississippi to solve a mystery. The suspected hammerer himself was wandering among the primroses in the garden. And my aunt wanted me to stay indoors and miss it all.

I raced to find my own footwear.

"You cannot possibly wear those godforsaken boots," whispered Aunt Kitty as she felt under her bed for her satin slippers. "It is time you get rid of those noisy clodhoppers. Do you have no other options?"

I finished pulling on my boots and stood tall in the center of the room. Tugging my own robe around me, I tried to make my eyes as fiery as hers tended to get.

"My daddy gave me two things in this world, Aunt Kitty," I said testily, "his name and his boots. One I parted with happily. But the other will have to be pulled off my cold, dead body when my soul has departed for the Heavenly By-and-By."

Aunt Kitty got to her feet with a *hmmph*, but she spoke no more against my boots. She slipped into her own shoes, and off we sneaked along the creaky hallway and down the wide, carpeted staircase. Aunt Kitty was in such a hurry, we left the oil lamp and the poker behind.

The unlit house was silent except for the ticking of a grandfather clock somewhere on the first floor. When we stepped onto the back porch, the whir of the cicadas made us both jump. We froze like a couple of stone statues for a moment, listening for Mr. Drysdale to catch us prowling. But the yard was quiet.

Aunt Kitty glided down the steps without a sound and moved along the path like a ghostly apparition. Her long chestnut hair was undone from its knot and swung wildly at her shoulders. I recalled Mr. Pinkerton's request that I play the role of a ghost on this adventure, and I half wondered if that's what we were doing now, haunting the garden like we were.

My aunt pulled me close as we passed along the jasmine, explaining in a hushed voice what she thought was Mr. Drysdale's motivation for doing the killing. She said Detective Webster had become friends with him, and Mr. Drysdale talked endlessly about buying new land.

"I suspect it all amounts to greed," she whispered. "If it was, indeed, Mr. Drysdale who killed the bank teller and stole the money, he has likely hidden it. And that one hundred and thirty thousand could be in this backyard, where he is visiting it *right now*."

My eyes scanned the shrubbery ahead of us for any sign of him.

"I wish you'd have brought a rope, Aunt Kitty," I complained softly. "What will we do once we catch him? I've been teaching myself to pinkie whistle. I might be able to roust someone up to help us."

Aunt Kitty ignored me and kept on walking.

"Or what if Mr. Drysdale catches us following him out here?" I pressed. "How will we explain ourselves? He ain't likely to believe we're stargazers."

"We will not let ourselves get caught," Aunt Kitty declared. And because she couldn't let a moment pass without setting me straight, she added, "And the proper word is *isn't*, not *ain't*. Mind your grammar, even in times of distress."

We inched on along the path, our arms entwined, until we caught sight of the white nightshirt up ahead in a clearing. I heard the babble of what must have been a small stream, and in the faint moonlight I could see Mr. Drysdale standing right at the water's edge.

I reached up for the nearest branch of the magnolia tree above us, and I quietly snapped it in two, leaving a heavy blossom at the end to dangle like a fragrant chandelier. It would be a marker for me and Aunt Kitty tomorrow, to let us know right where he was lurking.

As Mr. Drysdale slowly turned around, I saw his face. It was as if he were wearing a mask—his eyes were emotionless and seemed not to register anything around him. Aunt Kitty and I ducked behind the nearest shrub to escape his notice, and he passed us by, oblivious to our presence.

Hours later, when the morning light splintered through the bedroom curtains, I could barely lift my head from the pillow. I was so tired by the night's adventures, my temples were pounding and my eyes felt puffy. And frankly, having grown accustomed to the silky cradle over at the hotel, I'd found it hard to sleep on plain old cotton sheets again. My body was dog tired.

But there was Aunt Kitty, pacing the wooden floors like a nervous cat and mumbling to herself. She was already dressed in her red plaid gown, and her hair was twisted back in its usual perfect bun.

"I cannot work out what he was doing in the garden last night," she said to me, like I'd been part of her conversation all morning. "He walked right past the cobwebs and branches as if he didn't see them."

Her brows were pinched together like a couple of busy knitting needles, and she kept on trying to make sense of the nighttime garden scene. "Your response to nocturnal noises was normal—a gasp here, a jump of surprise there. But Mr. Drysdale did none of that. It was as if he were..."

"...sound asleep as he walked," I said with a yawn, trying to fill in the gaps.

Aunt Kitty suddenly stopped her pacing and spun around to face me.

"Walking in his sleep, that's it! Excellent observation, Penelope," she said brightly. Then she pulled on her questionable feathered bonnet and headed for the door. "He's a somnambulist. We've got to meet with Detective Webster and Mr. Pinkerton immediately. Get dressed as fast as you can and tell Mrs. Drysdale I'm recovered enough for a brief stroll into town."

And as the door clicked shut, I pushed the fireplace poker off the bed and pulled the lace pillow over my head with a groan. Because *somnambulist* was going to be in my next vocabulary lesson, I just knew it.

Chapter 25

❧

In Which I Tell Jemma What I Can

October 3, 1860

Dear Jemma,

Tagging along with the Pickled Onion
has become more of a thrill than I'd first
anticipated. I will admit there is still the
tedium of being forced to do arithmetic
until my mind aches. And the vocabulary
drills often make me want to give up
speaking aloud for the rest of my days. But
when I am assisting the Pickled Onion, as

in recent days, my heart seems to thump faster in my chest.

I believe I can help her, but I must be courageous and smart at the same time, which makes me feel like I am a juggler from the circus. Sometimes I think you could be more of an aid to her, what with all your talents. I bet you already know how to track footprints in the dirt. What about tie a rope into a handcuff knot? Whistle with your pinkies? Those are skills I believe every girl should possess.

I think I understand why the Pickled Onion likes her job so much. While I have to be mindful not to spill her beans, here's what I have observed. From what I see, she is challenged every day with a new adventure. She must rely on her wits a great deal. And did I mention, there is no cooking, scrubbing, or tending to babes?

The Pickled Onion even gets to
XBMYY ZK XZYLWZYMY!*

I've been thinking hard about you and the Maple Tree and our families. Do you think you could explain more about what happened when you left us? Was my daddy with you that night? I have more questions rattling around my head than answers, and I think you can help me.

                      Very truly your friend,
                      Nell

* X=D, Y=S, and Z=I

Chapter 26

In Which Aunt Kitty Braves a Nighttime Haunting, and I Encounter a Ghastly Ghost

Late that night Aunt Kitty sneaked into Mr. Drysdale's bedroom while he slept. She didn't carry a serving tray of tea and cakes or any such refreshment. She carried a vial of blood.

Blood obtained, I observed to her repeatedly, through illicit means. Had I known when I taught her the finer points of gunmanship that she would use it to deliberately slay an innocent chipmunk, I never would have shown her how to pull the trigger. She said it was all in the name of stopping Evil in its tracks. But now and again, I had my doubts about Mr. Pinkerton's detectives and the lengths they were willing to go to in order to catch a criminal.

What if Mr. Drysdale were as innocent as that chipmunk? How could Aunt Kitty justify her antics?

But like any good detective, she could be very sly when she wanted something. So she tried to convince me the chipmunk was rabid.

"I'm once again to the garden tonight," she panted, upon returning to our room, the vial of chipmunk blood half as full as when she'd left. "Detective Webster said I need to be ready for another nighttime ramble. This time, Penelope, I expect you to stay put upstairs and observe from the safety of this room."

When midnight chimed on the grandfather clock, just as the night before, our sleepwalker soon emerged from his room, padded down the long hallway, and again slipped into the back garden.

Aunt Kitty slipped right along behind him.

And just as the night before, I was not about to be left behind.

I did not want to miss a moment of this escapade, so I pressed in close to my aunt as we crept along the path beside the shrubbery. But perhaps I was a bit too eager,

217

as I bumped into her more than a few times. "I appreciate that you are no squeamish child. But if you do not give me a bit more space to breathe, I will have you go sit among the rhododendrons."

I let out a long sigh and shoved my hands into the pockets of my robe. But I kept close pace with her every step, eagerly watching for our sleepwalker.

"Aunt," I choked, barely able to get the words out of my mouth. "Look at Mr. Drysdale there! His nightshirt is bloody!"

"Of course it is! It's chipmunk blood, and I put it there myself. We are trying to scare a confession out of the man. Now hush!" And she told me to wait where I stood, which I was not about to do. I stayed by her side like a burr in a horse's hoof.

Aunt Kitty, and me right along with her, tiptoed out to the center of the wide yard and began pouring drops of the chipmunk blood along the path Mr. Drysdale had taken from the house. Then we slipped back among the shrubbery once again.

He was just ahead of us, walking down toward the gently bubbling stream. I felt around in the leaves above us until I found the snapped magnolia branch.

I knew we were at the same spot we'd come to the night before.

Mr. Drysdale paced back and forth like a nervous dog guarding her pups. Then suddenly he waded into the water a few feet and began feeling around along the sandy banks. Something about his pacing and his preoccupied manner reminded me of Mrs. Maroney at her cellar door, guarding where she'd hidden her loot. And that's when I realized we must be near Mr. Drysdale's stolen money.

I tapped Aunt Kitty's shoulder and whispered this into her ear. I could practically see the big pirate X that marked the spot—his ill-gotten treasure lay buried right where his dreams were leading him.

The cold water must have revived his senses, because all at once Mr. Drysdale seemed to come awake with a start. Aunt Kitty and I dove behind another rhododendron bush and observed as he stumbled back onto the shore. He wore a befuddled expression and sputtered at his bloodied nightshirt.

Suddenly a twig snapped not five steps away from him. And I realized not only were there three of us in the yard now, but a fourth figure had emerged beside an ancient tree and was gazing back at us. And when it stepped into the clearing, I saw blood spilling down its head and onto its shoulders, the very picture I'd imagined over and over in my mind of the poor, murdered bank teller.

I tugged on Aunt Kitty's arm to alert her. But she'd spied the ghost as well and was pressing her finger to her lips to keep me quiet. Because Mr. Drysdale had seen it, too.

"No," came Mr. Drysdale's anguished denials. "No, it cannot be you!"

And then he took off running through the bushes across the yard, his wet nightshirt flapping in the light of the crescent moon. From behind us came more snapping of twigs. Aunt Kitty and I spun to face the latest danger, though I wasn't sure about the wisdom of turning our backs on the ghost.

"Good work, Mrs. Warne," came a man's voice, thick with a Scottish lilt. Immediately I knew it was Mr. Pinkerton. "This place reminds me of the moors—it's full of banshees!"

Then Mr. Pinkerton stepped over and shook hands with the ghostly figure, offering hearty congratulations. "Very convincing, Mr. Green," he said in a hushed voice. "You look remarkably like the dead bank teller himself, I believe. Mr. Bangs would be impressed to see your handiwork."

"And Nell, you're quite brave, too—for a *ghoul*," came Detective Webster's jolly, joking whisper on the other side of me. He gave my ribs a playful jab with his elbow. "Drysdale doesn't stand a *ghost* of a chance with you around."

The bloody specter greeted them all—first Mr. Pinkerton, Detective Webster, and finally Aunt Kitty— then he stepped over toward me with a friendly nod of his gory head.

"Nice to meet you, Miss Warne," he said, tipping his bloodstained cap as if we were at a Sunday picnic. Dropping his voice to a whisper, he added, "You're mighty tough. Most folks would be letting loose like a screech owl to see me in my costume. I'm real impressed, I am."

I shook his hand and tried to ignore the red goop that was smeared in his hair and down the back of his head. We stepped over toward the banks of the stream as we chatted, almost like he was a regular chum and not some phantom from the underworld.

"Are you another detective?" I asked, trying to

make friendly conversation. "Or are you just a sort of"—and here I paused, searching for what to call him—"demon for hire?"

Mr. Green grinned and let out a cheerful snort, which seemed at odds with his gruesome appearance. He said he was just helping Mr. Pinkerton out tonight, but he was leaving on the morning train for New Orleans.

"I'm taking a job in a fancy hotel there called the Saint Charles," he said. "You wouldn't know it to look at me now, but most days I'm a cook."

I remembered the plates of warm *Macaroni with Fromage* from the hotel with Aunt Kitty, and I could feel my mouth start to water.

"That's where we should dig," Aunt Kitty announced, ever mindful of the case at hand. "We believe Mr. Drysdale's dreams were leading him to his hidden treasure. I'll bet it is buried right there, where Penelope is standing."

And after nearly an hour or so of digging, performed alternately by Detective Webster and Mr. Green, the five of us heard a sudden scraping. Mr. Green's shovel had struck a trunk. After a bit more digging, he and Detective Webster hoisted the discovery out of the pit.

It was a small rectangular box with a sturdy lock in front. But a few well-placed jabs from the shovel got past that, and Mr. Pinkerton lifted the lid.

"Good gravy," I whispered.

"You can say that again, Nell," gasped Mr. Green.

"She's Penelope," corrected Aunt Kitty. "We're still undercover."

"Looks as if it's all here," judged Mr. Pinkerton, taking a quick inventory of the paper and coins. "The murderer didn't have the courage to spend it."

As we returned the dug-up riverbank to its former condition, tamping down the muddy area where the treasure had lain, Mr. Pinkerton and my aunt pondered the next step.

"We have evidence now," I said, joining them. "But what about an eyewitness?"

"I'm afraid the only witness to this murder was the bank teller himself—now deceased," Aunt Kitty replied.

"Then what do we need to solve the case?" I asked, worried that Mr. Drysdale might still slip away, only to hammer again.

"What we need, Nell—er, Penelope—is a confession," Mr. Pinkerton declared, running a hand through his wild brown beard. "I believe one final push from our ghost will scare it out of him."

The ghostly, ghastly Mr. Green nodded politely at Mr. Pinkerton but reminded him that he would be on tomorrow's eight-o'clock train bound for New Orleans. He wouldn't be around to do another night-time haunting.

"Of course, that's where our substitute comes in," Mr. Pinkerton said, tugging some more on that over-grown beard of his. "And it looks as if we have one of comparable height to Mr. Green."

Suddenly I noticed that Mr. Pinkerton was star-ing at the top of my head. Detective Webster was, too, along with Aunt Kitty, though she had that tight, pickled-onion face again. I slapped my hands up there in case a bat was flitting around my hair, and I bumped my elbow into Mr. Green's ear beside me. We turned to face each other, and I noticed we were just about nose to nose.

"Oh, you cannot be serious, Mr. P—" began Aunt Kitty in protest.

"Mr. Pinkerton," interrupted Detective Webster with a wide grin, "I think she's perfect for the job."

"She's just a girl," my aunt sputtered. "You said so yourself on the train!"

"Just a girl?" retorted Detective Webster, the smile never leaving his face. "There's no such thing as *just a girl*, is there, Mrs. Warne? There's Nell, and Nell Warne can do great things!"

Mr. Pinkerton waved at the two of them to hush, and then he fixed his fierce eyes on me. "That's what makes her perfect for the job, Mrs. Warne. The girl has a certain theatricality about her that I find remarkable.

"So what do you say, lass?" he whispered in that lolling way of his. "Are you up for it?"

I shot a look at Aunt Kitty, who was gazing skyward for some sort of divine counsel. Detective Webster stood beside her, appearing every bit the devilish imp. Then I peeked beside me at Mr. Green's ghoulish costume as the hammered bank teller—at the bloody gunk that streamed from his head and over his shoulders, and at the gory, red-stained jacket. He was a repulsive mess, a true fiend if ever there was one. He was, in a word, disgusting.

And he was also the key to cracking this case.

"Mr. Pinkerton," I said, "it would be an honor."

Chapter 27

❧❦❧

In Which I Scare Up
a Confession

It wasn't until the end of breakfast the next day when Mr. Drysdale made an appearance at the table, his hair wet from what I assumed was a long scrubbing in the bathtub. He was pale and jumpy, his hands fluttering here and there like two hummingbirds. He had spent a good part of the morning walking in and out of the house, pacing the backyard, then rushing off to his room and back. Surely he was trying to understand the trail of blood and his encounter with the ghostly bank teller.

Finally, he announced that he had an appointment

downtown at the bank at noon. He said something about wanting to close an account.

Aunt Kitty and I got to our feet like a couple of startled jackrabbits. Pushing our chairs back, we both grabbed our bonnets, blathered something to Mrs. Drysdale about getting some fresh air, and skittered out the back door. Our horses were still saddled from our morning ride, so we jumped right onto their backs and gave hearty "hee-yahs." Aunt Kitty set the pace at a gallop as we made our way down the tree-lined back roads for town.

"We've got to get you into disguise," she called over her shoulder. "We'll go straight to Mr. Pinkerton's office. He'll have the costume there. We can't waste a minute!"

When we reached the small room Mr. Pinkerton had rented over the post office, Detective Webster let us in. We quickly gave them all the news they needed, knowing Mr. Drysdale was surely preparing for his meeting at the bank.

"Then let's get Nell here into her uniform as fast as we can," Mr. Pinkerton directed. "I shall go pay a call on the bank president and meet the rest of you there."

And as he clomped down the staircase toward the street, Aunt Kitty took a seat at the table and began mixing up the red stage makeup. I stepped to the wardrobe in the back of the room, where Detective Webster was unfolding the bloodied bank-teller costume. I always knew him to be playful and sly, so I wasn't ready for the serious expression his face was wearing.

"You've been a good assistant to Mrs. Warne," he began, his voice low enough for just my ears. "But what you're doing now is a help to all of us. We've never had so much on the line. I hope you're not afraid."

I shook my head. I wasn't afraid of too many things in this life. Just loneliness. But I wasn't feeling much of that now, not since I had begun tagging along on Aunt Kitty's adventures. That heavy sack of sorrows I'd been carrying around for so long, well, it was feeling a bit lighter. And now, portraying a phantom—perhaps this might help me put some of my own ghosts to rest.

"Be fearless, Nell," he whispered, "in everything you do. Fearless." And with a quick punch to my shoulder, he was back to being the same old Detective Webster again.

I shut the door to the tiny back room to change in

private. Aunt Kitty came in a few minutes later with the stage makeup and a comb.

"Let me slick back your hair with this pomade." She tugged a comb across my head as I fastened the last of the vest buttons on the gruesome costume. I sat down in a stiff chair and pulled my boots on, pondering the task ahead. To scare a confession out of this dubious Mr. Drysdale, I had but one speaking part. And it was simple—a low and mournful moan.

I practiced it a few times to get it right.

"Ooowwwwwww," I tried.

It needed more *ah* to get going.

"Ahhhhhoooooowwwww."

I used my stomach muscles to add a bit more heft to the groan. Some might call me a perfectionist, but there's nothing wrong with trying to do a job right. As I began another round of wailing, Aunt Kitty heaved a sigh that let me know she'd had just about enough.

I tugged Mr. Green's messy hat onto my head, and I caught sight of my reflection in the window glass. I was a horrifying mess! Aunt Kitty had applied the red stage makeup in a gloopy pile on the side and back of my head, and it looked unpleasantly real. As I straightened the bank-teller jacket, I noticed more red goop on my shoulders and one arm. It was so gruesome as to be humorous, and I couldn't suppress the urge to smile at my appearance.

Aunt Kitty came to stand right behind me, taking in my reflection, too.

"Mr. Pinkerton seems to think you have the right spirit," she began, fussing over a stream of fake blood on my shoulder. "I want you to know that you will not be in danger at any moment, Nell. If anything goes awry, we will all be there for you. Do not panic."

I started to ask her if she'd ever seen me panic in all the time we'd been together, but I didn't want to argue with her now. Not when she'd finally come around to the notion of me portraying the ghostly bank teller.

"I could tell you weren't too happy last night in the garden. You don't think I'm good enough to be a detective's assistant. But that's all right," I said, more to comfort myself than her. "You'll see. There's a job to be done, Aunt Kitty, and I'm the right one to do it."

I adjusted my tie and asked her how I looked.

"Dreadful," she replied. But when I looked at her

eyes in the window glass, I thought I saw a smile there. "And stop calling me Kitty."

Right about then, it was time to leave for the bank. Aunt Kitty opened a wide black umbrella to cover my head from the curious eyes of the townsfolk. And Detective Webster strolled right in front of me, creating a burly barrier between my unsightly appearance and any passersby on the sidewalk to the bank.

Mr. Pinkerton arrived moments behind us, along with four men Aunt Kitty said were the bank president and directors. They nodded to my aunt and me, eyeing us both curiously. I wasn't sure if it was because of the tortured bird roosting atop my aunt's bonnet, or my uncommon costume—or if it was because they'd never met lady detectives before. I squared my shoulders like Aunt Kitty was doing and paraded past them as regally as Queen Victoria heading to her throne.

Detective Webster warned them that Mr. Drysdale's carriage was likely to arrive at any moment, so all of them took their places. Aunt Kitty and I tucked into an alcove behind an enormous statue of Lady Justice while Detective Webster hid himself behind a flag. We made sure to have a clear view of the proceedings but not be seen; if Mr. Drysdale spied us conspiring together, he might catch on to our scheme.

The tall front door opened a bit later, letting a triangle of bright daylight fall upon the marble floor. A hush swept over the bank as Mr. Drysdale stepped inside, his eyes blinking a few moments as he adjusted to the dimmer gaslight of the bank's ornate lobby. He was accompanied by a heavyset man.

"That must be his lawyer," Detective Webster whispered.

Mr. Pinkerton and the bank directors greeted Mr. Drysdale and his companion, and they all began a conversation that I could not follow from my vantage point. I'd gotten myself distracted by thinking about the fairness of what we were doing. What if Mr. Drysdale had done no wrong? Was it right of me to terrify the poor man?

I scratched my head as these thoughts poked at my conscience, and then I saw the bloody goop on my fingertips. Maybe he was innocent.

But then again, maybe not.

Aunt Kitty stepped aside and nodded for me to pass, giving my arm a quick squeeze.

"Now is your moment to shine."

I gave her a squeeze back, then stepped out from behind the statue.

Mr. Pinkerton and the other men were arranged with their backs to me in a horseshoe around Mr. Drysdale, which somehow afforded our suspect the only clear view of my antics. As the others talked on, Mr. Drysdale fixed on me with a look of such terror, I thought his two eyes could have popped out of his head and splattered onto the marble floor like a pair of goose eggs.

I approached their group with a few staggering steps, my arms outstretched before me like a member of the walking dead. I expected Mr. Drysdale to recoil backward, perhaps even turn and run for the door. But instead he stood frozen to the ground as if his feet were blocks of ice. The only part of his buggy-eyed body to move was his jaw, which flapped open and shut but produced no sound.

I felt a few coins shift in the pocket of my bloodied

bank teller's jacket, so I pulled out what I found. There were a few bills tucked inside as well, so I decided to add my own theatrical flourish. I let the money spill through my fingers as I emitted the low and mournful groan that I'd been rehearsing.

"Aaaahhhh-ooowwwwwaaahhh!"

And that did the trick.

"You again?" Mr. Drysdale shouted, finally pulling his eyes from my ghostly form. "I can't take it anymore! I am guilty! *Guilty!* I'm haunted each and every night by you! This money is cursed!"

When we boarded the train back to Chicago that evening, I was still walking on air. Aunt Kitty may have heard enough, but my ears never tired of listening to Mr. Pinkerton and Detective Webster compliment my performance. I tried to keep the satisfied grin off my face, but it was no use.

As the wheels started turning, I scooched up against the window, tucking myself in behind my reading. While I wished I could share my adventures with Jemma on the journey home, I couldn't wait to get back to the boardinghouse and the envelopes waiting for me there.

I set my cigar box full of Jemma's old correspondences on the bench beside me, and I opened a few newspapers scavenged from the depot. There were stories of the Apache Wars in the Wild West, a new circus act called a flying trapeze, and Abraham Lincoln arguing that Kansas should be a free state and not slave. I breathed a happy sigh, letting my cup of happiness runneth over as the train picked up speed for Chicago. Not only did I have a new dress and a thrilling new story—I had the good company of Jemma's letters, the *Mississippian and State Gazette*, and "Honest Abe" Lincoln to see me home.

Chapter 28

In Which Jemma Makes Me Cry

October 13, 1860

Dear Nell,

I wish you could tell me more about the Pickled Onion and what she is doing—and why she gets to wear costumes, if that's what your last cipher said!

I like you sharing what you can. But most of all, I love hearing about that food. The pecan pie makes my mouth water. Have you ever heard of a dessert called iced cream? I was down at the store buying some flour for Mama last week when I listened in on some old men talking about it. They say it marries right with pie.

I don't want anyone around here to know, but I'm going to try to make "maerc deci allinav" as a surprise for Mama soon. That might sound like one of your fancy Italian foods, but you'll have to turn it around in your head to figure it out.

Maybe someday I'll make some for you, too. I wonder when that will happen. For now, my memories of our last day together and that big weeping willow are still clear in my mind. Do you know why we had to leave? I think I should tell you some more, because it has to do with the Maple Tree.

You and I were so young and eager to get away from the old folks, we didn't hear all the things that happened on the farms. But I think you might recall my uncle Ezekiel and his family. There were eight of them, and they kept to themselves on the other side of the river from us. We saw them at Christmas and Easter, and that was about all. They had two sets of twin boys, so things were always noisy and messy whenever they were around.

But my uncle Ezekiel was friendly, and he's the one who gave me those baby ducks. You know how much I loved my ducks, so you can imagine how much I loved Uncle Ezekiel.

About a month before we left, I woke up one morning to the sound of the Maple Tree crying. It wasn't a quiet kind of crying either—he was howling at heaven and shaking all over. He'd just found out about Uncle Ezekiel's family, and the hurt in him opened up like a river. Tears poured out of him when he told me Uncle Ezekiel and Aunt Liza and all their six babies had been stolen by some slave hunters.

Mama says your daddy told her it was all right, that we'd be fine since we'd been farming the same fields in Chemung County since the Maple Tree was a baby. Your daddy said over and over not to worry, that he knew ways to keep us safe. But the Maple Tree said it didn't make any difference. Some folks don't see a black man as a man at all. He said some folks just see him as property.

I guess maybe for those slave hunters, they saw a lot of property in Chemung County that needed to be taken back down South.

It wasn't too much later, and we were gone just like Ezekiel. Only Mama and me and the babies went north instead of south. Your daddy probably told you all about it, what with his brother and all.

When my mind gets to wandering off, like when I'm at church (don't tell Mama), I think about Uncle Ezekiel and his babies and where they all are now. I catch every word those old gossips say at the chicken dinners after services. I know that Uncle Ezekiel and his babies aren't together anymore. That slaves get sold off to the highest bidder. That nobody thinks twice about tearing twins apart from each other.

Sometimes my ears burn when I hear such things. And I feel like running out the church door and across our fields, running all the way to where the Maple Tree is so I can help. I even dream I'm running, some nights, my legs so fast that I begin to fly. And I am one of those blue herons, with mighty wings spread out wide and far.

I know Mama says not to pay attention to all that talk. But I think the most important thing we can do is pay attention, especially when what we hear hurts so much. How else will we know the work to be done?

I need to ask something of you now. I need you to tell the Maple Tree something if you find him. It's too important to turn into a cipher, so I'll put it to you straight. Tell him I'm coming. I don't know when or how, but someday soon, I'm coming.

Your friend forever and ever,
Jemma

Chapter 29

In Which Aunt Kitty Gets a Taste of Current Events, and I Get a Taste of Something Unsettling

When we returned to Chicago and our familiar room in the boardinghouse, I did not exactly dive into my lumpy bed like a pig into a mud bath. But I was happy to be back in familiar territory. While the Drysdale case had been exciting for its silk sheets and fancy costumes, I knew I would sleep better at night without fireplace tools under my pillow.

Our daily meals were once again taken at Mrs. Wigginbottom's crowded table, the memories of the

Mississippi hotel's swirly menu and sinfully good food fading like steam from a teakettle. And while there could be no open display of celebrating for Aunt Kitty and myself after our work on the murder case, we both were feeling the satisfaction of another mystery solved. I detected a touch of laughter in my aunt's manner that first evening at supper as she helped pass the steaming bowls of stew down the line to the other boarders. And I felt a warm glow inside, even before taking a single bite of our hot meal.

It took only a few gruff words from our landlady to snuff out that candle of joy shining within me.

"I assume you'll get back to your marketing tomorrow, Nell," she began dramatically, her jowly hound-dog cheeks flapping as she ladled out bowl after bowl of fragrant stew. "It wasn't easy fetching the things for supper, what with my knees and swollen feet. I had to resort to drastic measures to keep the house fed."

I felt a twinge of guilt that I'd neglected my obligations to Mrs. Wigginbottom for so long. Those useless bachelors, Mr. Hummer and Mr. Slammer, obviously provided little help in my absence. I gave an apologetic smile to the others around the table, knowing that without my bargaining with the butcher and the produce seller, the meals here were probably pitiful. I promised her I would get back to it tomorrow, and thankfully, the conversation flowed again as a heaping bowl was plunked down before me.

"Did you read this, Aunt Kitty?" I asked, turning back to my newspaper and trying to ignore my aunt's reproachful eye. I knew she did not approve of such distractions at the dining table. But it made me twitchy not to be caught up on the current events of the day. So I went on reading and tried to ignore the pickled-onion face she was giving me. "They've gone and nominated Mr. Lincoln for president! And he just might win this contest."

I noticed the sweet newlywed Mrs. Nash had stopped sipping her coffee and was hanging on my every word. She lived in one of the pricey rooms on the first floor with her husband, Mr. Nash, who worked as a photographer on State Street. I wanted desperately to visit his shop and have our photographs taken, but I feared bringing it up again with Aunt Kitty.

"Go on, Nell," urged Mrs. Nash gently, "keep reading. I may not have a vote, but I do have an interest."

I rustled the pages of the *Chicago Press & Tribune* and cleared my throat importantly.

"This dispatch is dated from September thirtieth over in Springfield. It says folks were crowded round to hear him give a speech about slavery in Kansas, and 'a fine Glee Club entertained the audience with vocal music.' Sounds nice, don't it?"

I heard a little *hmmph* from Aunt Kitty's direction, and I could not tell whether she was troubled by glee clubs or my slip in grammar. I decided to continue with my reading and ignore her.

"It goes on to say the speaker predicted the triumphant election of Abraham Lincoln and Hannibal Hamlin in next month's election 'by a splendid popular majority.'"

"Well, I'll be," said Mr. Nash with surprise. "We could have an abolitionist in the White House. What will come of things?"

"He'll never get elected," huffed that irksome Mr. Slammer. "The nation would split in two if Lincoln won. There's plenty who won't hear of giving slaves their freedom."

Aunt Kitty seemed to sense a fight coming, so she

snatched the paper from my hands and ordered me to eat, shutting down any chance for a great debate. I turned my attention to my supper and sniffed curiously, poking at the brown hunks with my spoon.

"Nell, have you seen the orange tabby around lately?" inquired Mrs. Nash sweetly. "I used to see you feeding milk to that darling cat on the back porch after your market trips. But where has it gone?"

Mrs. Wigginbottom suddenly dropped her ladle into the stew pot with such a crash, it silenced the group.

"What is in tonight's stew, Mrs. Wigginbottom?" choked Mr. Slammer, his beardless face crinkled like a prune. "Supper is especially, *ahem,* flavorful this evening."

"Yes," agreed Mr. Hummer politely, but not daring to take another bite, "I don't recognize this as mutton or ham. It has an unusual taste."

Mrs. Wigginbottom became flustered by the attention her stew was getting, and she lumbered off to the kitchen saying she was after more cabbage and bread. When she returned, red-faced and a little sweaty, I felt something click in my mind.

"You mentioned 'drastic measures' a moment ago," I began, visions of the orange tomcat racing through my head. "What does that mean?"

All eyes around the table shot from Mrs. Wigginbottom's flushed face to the bowls of hot stew before them. And in quick succession, spoons clinked onto plates as diner after diner slid the meal away.

"I'd say the cat's got her tongue," joked Mr. Slammer. He looked around the table for a laugh, but his timing could not have been worse. He cleared his throat and began fussing with his napkin.

"Pass the cabbage, please," croaked Mr. Hummer after a few moments of heavy silence. "More Indian cornbread, anyone?"

Chapter 30

In Which I Try to Recall Jemma's Last Night

November 10, 1860

Dear Jemma,

I loved reading about the surprise dessert you're making for your mama. But the part in your letter about the Maple Tree and all his sorrows made me weep like a baby. I don't recall much about your uncle Ezekiel, but I did love those ducks, too. I imagine the Maple Tree never got over the hurt of losing his brother. How could he? I remember my own brothers in my prayers every night.

I do not recall much about the time you left. I just know I missed you something awful when my daddy told me you were gone. I thought I'd done something to hurt your feelings, since you never said good-bye and we never got to exchange presents or spit in our hands and seal our friendship. But now I know there was no time for saying good-bye.

After they buried the Pickled Onion's husband, my daddy got real quiet. He never talked about that night, so I don't know what happened. I only heard dribs and drabs from gossips around town. And I wasn't allowed to go to the funeral— Daddy thought it was bad luck to have a child so close to the Grim Reaper. But still, it didn't stop all the dying that was to come—my mama passing, followed so quickly by my brothers. And then Daddy himself.

My question to you now is, How did it happen? Tell me all you can about how the Pickled Onion's husband came to his tragic end, if you feel that you won't put anyone in danger.

I'm mighty grateful for your help piecing together this mystery. And I will do all I can to help you, too, and tell the Maple Tree what needs telling. I don't know if the Pickled Onion's work will take me to see Phil O'Dell again. But I sure can try to find a way to get there.

And I believe someday you will, too—you just have to be extra safe about it.

I wonder if the news has reached you there in Canada. Abraham Lincoln won the contest for president of the United States. And folks say he intends to put an end to slavery. Can you imagine that? What a day it would be for you and your mama and the Maple Tree.

I dreamed last night that you came here to Chicago, and we rode my mule,

Whiskey, past Potter Palmer's emporium and ate fried bread on Lake Street. You sold stacks of your pies and made more money than could fit into your purse.

Very truly your friend,
Nell

Chapter 31

In Which Aunt Kitty Tries to Rid Herself of Me, and I Meet the Reason Why

H elp me find the wool stockings," Aunt Kitty ordered one freezing February morning a few months later. Her voice was muffled by the fact that she was deep within the wardrobe. When she finally emerged, she was lugging a heavy woolen cloak. "Baltimore will be just as cold as Chicago, so I'll need lots of warm things for my stay there."

I told Aunt Kitty I'd help her pack, but I could hardly pull myself away from my newspaper. Now that "Honest Abe" Lincoln had won the presidency, the South was in a dither. Every day featured another story about South Carolina or Mississippi trying to tear apart the Union. Mr. Lincoln hadn't even sat down in his big presidential chair, and already seven states were breaking away, forming their own confederacy.

I was about to start sharing this news with Aunt Kitty when a knock at the door interrupted me. I dashed over to see who was there, half expecting to find a sweaty Mrs. Wigginbottom propping herself up against the doorframe after her exhausting climb to our floor. Instead I found an apple-cheeked woman with the palest blue eyes I'd ever seen.

"I'm calling on Mrs. Warne, please," she said softly, her manner of speech slow and deliberate.

My aunt stepped over to the door, still holding the wool cloak in her arms, and shook the woman's black-gloved hand. "Miss Lawton, what a delight. Please come in and meet my niece.

"Nell, this is our newest detective, Miss Hattie Lawton."

We received so few visitors to our room, I wasn't sure what I was supposed to do. I gestured toward the rocking chair beside the fire, but then I wondered if that was too informal. So I made a dash for the straight-backed chair beside the small table, but I caught my toe on the spare logs at the fireplace and sent them tumbling. As I bent down to collect them, I bumped the sewing basket off Aunt Kitty's chair and heard the sound of a hundred tiny straight pins *ping* their way across my aunt's freshly swept floor.

"It's a pleasure, Nell," this Miss Lawton said, and she smiled so warmly, I stopped my fussing and shook her hand. Her pale eyes were almond-shaped and wide set beneath two slender black eyebrows. And with her smooth black hair swept over her ears, she reminded me of a graceful cat. "Mrs. Warne has told me a great deal about you."

She has?

Now what was I supposed to think of that? I forgot all about Hattie Lawton and the straight pins for a moment and stared dumbly at my aunt, wondering what in the world she would have to say about me to a stranger.

"Your timing is perfect, Miss Lawton. I was just having Nell assist me with the packing for tomorrow. Mr. Pinkerton is not one for waiting around. Especially not on this mission."

"What sort of escapade is it this time?" I asked, putting away the pins and hoping I'd be included. "Will there be danger? Murder? Treachery?"

"Possibly two of the three, Nell," Aunt Kitty called from the back room, her arms in the wardrobe again and digging so quickly that she seemed like some sort of high-strung gopher. Finally she popped her head up, then passed a few gowns out to Hattie Lawton. "But on this case I cannot divulge our plans. Secrecy is too important. It is a matter of life and death."

Whose life and whose death?

I shot a look over at Miss Lawton and felt my cheeks burn with embarrassment. Why wouldn't Aunt Kitty trust me? Hadn't I proven myself to be faithful? Hadn't I worked hard to earn my place beside her, as a detective's assistant? I thought back on the part I played in the fortune-teller case, as the book peddler in the Maroney adventure, and as the haunting, hammered bank teller in the Drysdale affair. I was so good, I could have been on Mr. Pinkerton's payroll myself, with Mr. Bangs worrying over my every need.

Suddenly my embarrassment turned to anger. Was I still a burden to her? I had tried to believe she was no longer plotting to ship me off somewhere. But the letter waiting for Aunt Kitty on the downstairs table yesterday, with HOME FOR THE FRIENDLESS written in tight script on the envelope's back, didn't help. I hadn't opened it, but then again I hadn't told her about it either. It was still under my mattress in the back room.

I wasn't about to hand over my own jail sentence.

"Fine, I don't want to know your secret," I snapped testily. I didn't care that Hattie Lawton was present to witness our disagreement. "I can stay here this time. I'm good enough at caring for myself. I don't need you around."

I snatched up Aunt Kitty's favorite bonnet and began running my fingers through the long pheasant feathers. I gave Miss Lawton a distrustful look, then hurled the silly hat onto the rocking chair.

Aunt Kitty came out of the small bedroom.

"As a matter of fact, you're right, Nell," she said. "You will stay behind this time. I've already arranged it with Mrs. Wigginbottom. She will watch after you while I am gone, for a fee, of course. I trust you will behave yourself."

Trust? My eyes burned into hers. How could she

even use that word, *trust*? When for a few dollars, she was willing to rid herself of me? Leave me in the care of that dodgy, despicable landlady?

Hattie Lawton stepped away to the corner of the room, as far from us as possible, and started busying herself with the gowns.

Suddenly I could see it all so clearly. My aunt was through with me. What good was I when she had this new detective—the beautiful, catlike Hattie Lawton— to replace me? And when she had the Home for the Friendless waiting to offer me a cold, filthy bed?

Storming past her into the bedroom, I pulled the cigar box out from underneath my mattress and flung the lid open.

"Do they teach trust at the Home for the Friendless?" I asked, emerging from the room and waving the letter toward her. My voice was dripping with a venom I didn't even know I possessed. But I found her secrets enraging. And knowing she didn't want me anymore, well, the hurt coiled up inside me like an asp. I wanted to strike and hurt her back.

"That is my letter," Aunt Kitty said, staring at the cream-colored envelope, MRS. KATE WARNE scrawled prettily across the front. She put out her hand for me to give it to her.

"Are there others with it?" she snapped.

Suddenly I felt ashamed as I pulled out four more envelopes—one from the Protestant Orphan Asylum, two from the Catholic home, and another from a place I'd never heard of—and laid them in her palm.

"I did inquire, Nell. I've heard the Home for the Friendless takes good care of the older girls, puts them to work tending to the younger ones. Surely one of these places would make a more suitable home than here," she said calmly, gesturing around our tiny two rooms but keeping her eyes locked on my face. "More suitable than what I can do for you, dashing off on a railcar toward peril at the drop of a hat."

"So why haven't you set me on their doorstep already?" I said, feeling the sting of tears in my eyes. "You can save yourself paying Mrs. Wigginbottom for me, like I'm some piece of old mutton."

"Because," she replied, tapping the stack of envelopes against her hand, "I have been awaiting their responses."

I caught my breath as if I'd been punched in the stomach. She'd certainly been busy.

"If you haven't noticed, Aunt Kitty, I'm just fine riding railcars toward peril."

Hattie Lawton was standing in the corner, looking uncomfortably at the two of us. "Detective work does sound exciting," she said vaguely, maybe in the hope of redirecting the conversation. But we were too far into our fighting to regard her.

"It's wrong to expose you to danger, Nell. So you cannot join me on this case. And as to the orphan asylums, well, I can scarcely afford to feed two mouths. I worry that I'm one step away from the poorhouse myself," she said, jabbing the iron poker into the fireplace and stirring the flames.

"At the Home for the Friendless, you will have security. Not only will you have a bed and three meals, you will be taught properly—sums and vocabulary, as well as virtues like respect, hard work, responsibility. And..." she added darkly, turning to face me. Her eyes shot straight to my brown boots. "Integrity."

There it was, that heavy cloud hanging in the air. Everything between us hinged on my daddy—my faith in him.

And Aunt Kitty's lack of it.

I heard my bedsprings squeak in the back room. Hattie Lawton must have decided to sit down in there and wait out this storm.

"You think I'm going to turn out like him, don't you?"

"I cannot look at your face and not see Cornelius Warne gazing back at me, Nell," she began, squeezing her eyes shut. "The gambling. The drink. The lies."

I reminded Aunt Kitty that I was not like him. Hadn't I proven myself to her? Couldn't she just put the past to rest and trust me?

"Trust you, Nell?" she snapped with a bitter laugh. "You've already deceived me by hiding these letters."

"But I am not him, Aunt Kitty—"

"Him, *him*! When Cornelius killed Matthew, he took everything from me, Nell. It is because of *him* that I am alone in the world."

Alone? That cut me deep. Sure, we were both haunted by the ghosts of Warne men. But we still had real, flesh-and-blood family walking this good green earth.

Each other.

"I would be grateful," I whispered through my hurt, "to be even half the man my daddy was."

"Well, the good news here," Aunt Kitty said, snatching the pheasant bonnet from the rocker and tugging it onto her head, "is that you are a woman."

And she picked up the black cloak, uttered something about the dry-goods store, and pulled the door shut behind her. I reached over and put my hand on the mantel and tried to calm my breathing. My eyes stung with tears, though I refused to let them fall.

Hattie Lawton emerged from the back room a few moments later and timidly came to stand near me at the fire. She ran her hand over the dresses draped on the parlor chair and peeked at my face. I think she was trying to read my expression.

"You should take those with you," I said, nodding at the gowns. "Take whatever clothes and woolens you might need. Baltimore winters can be mighty cold, they say."

Miss Lawton fingered the gowns, but she didn't budge from where she stood. Her eyes were locked on mine, and she patted my arm. "What can I do to help you?" she asked in her sweet, slow way.

"Don't worry about me," I said with a heavy sigh. "I'll pack my bags and be gone soon enough."

But Miss Lawton wouldn't hear of it, and she urged me to stay put and be a help to Mrs. Wigginbottom.

"Darling Nell," she said gently, taking one of my hands in her own, "I know you won't believe me when I tell you this, but your aunt cares for you deeply. You're all she talks about at our meetings—I feel as if I know you already.

"I come from a family of six girls, so believe me when I say it. Even though you're not getting along right now, you will again. The two of you are like sisters."

Sisters? I fought the urge to laugh. Miss Lawton said something about packing later, then she turned and headed for the door.

"If me and Aunt Kitty are like sisters," I whispered bitterly, my eyes fixed on the flames in the fireplace, "then I'd rather be alone."

As Hattie Lawton pulled the door shut behind her, I listened to the mantel clock ticking in the empty room.

Alone was exactly what I was.

Again.

Chapter 32

In Which Aunt Kitty Leads Me from the Plague

Wake up, Nell," came my aunt's voice the next morning. "You need to dress as quickly as possible. Get moving!"

I sat up groggily in my bed and tried to make sense of what I was hearing. Aunt Kitty stood beside me in her black wool cloak. Mrs. Wigginbottom's jowly face peered over my aunt's shoulder, looking red and weepy as she pressed a white hankie to her nose.

"Good heavens, she's not feverish, too, is she Mrs. Warne? Oh, the Angel of Death is upon us!"

"She is not feverish, Mrs. Wigginbottom. But I will

be if you do not stop your infernal wailing," snapped my aunt. "Now, if you please, get out of this room so the child can dress."

Once Mrs. Wigginbottom closed the door, I threw off my covers and stared at Aunt Kitty for some sort of explanation. Today was the day she was to depart for Baltimore with Mr. Pinkerton and the other detectives. And it was the day I was to start investigating a new living arrangement.

"I'll fetch your heavy coat and gloves, Nell. You throw on your checkered gown. We've got to get a move on if we're going to make the train."

"I'm not going to Baltimore with you, Aunt Kitty. Remember? You've already sold my soul to Mrs. Wigginbottom."

Aunt Kitty bristled at my words. But I didn't pay her any mind. She'd hurt me deeply yesterday, and I wasn't about to forgive or forget.

"The plans have changed, Nell. I want you coming with me. Now move swiftly."

"You seemed pretty dead set on leaving me behind yesterday," I said, still sitting where I was on the bed. I smoothed down my nightshirt and wiggled my toes within my thick wool socks. I was in no hurry to do her bidding. "What in the world could possibly have changed your mind this morning?"

"Measles. Down the hall from us. Now please get into your dress, Nell, before it's too late."

I stood up and padded over to the wooden wardrobe that held our clothes, but my mind was in a bit of shock. I'd read in the newspapers about cholera, typhoid, and all sorts of other plagues that afflicted our city. I wasn't so sure about measles.

Aunt Kitty seemed able to read my mind. And as I shimmied into my dress, she stuffed stockings and unmentionables into my carpetbag and explained what was happening at Mrs. Wigginbottom's boardinghouse.

"They discovered the body of that gentleman who resides at the end of our hallway just a few hours ago—"

"Mr. Hummer?" I shouted.

"No, the other one."

"Mr. Slammer! Is he dead?"

"Mind your manners, Nell," she scolded, handing me a comb and pointing toward the washbasin. "Yes, the unfortunate soul has succumbed. And that sweet

Mrs. Nash downstairs is burning with fever, too. It does not look good for her either, I fear. And so I feel that I cannot leave you amid such contagion. While my latest case may involve peril, I believe it would be far more dangerous for you to remain here."

She didn't have to say another word. With a few quick swipes of that comb, I was done with my preparations. I jumped into my boots, grabbed my carpetbag and the heavy wool coat, and we were on our way to the train depot.

"What am I to do with this brooch?" I asked, fumbling with a silly circular pin of blue silk ribbon the size of my fist. "Affix it to my bonnet?"

"That is to be worn on your gown," Aunt Kitty explained, slowly turning an identical one in her hands and scowling. "The Baltimore ladies are showing their sympathies with the slave-owning states by pinning these blue cockades to their breasts. It is the emblem of secession."

I stared across at her and blinked. What was that

word, *secession*? Had she said *succession*? As in one thing following another? Or *cessation*? Meaning something to cease?

"Another one for the vocabulary list, I see, Nell," my aunt said with a sigh, the railroad tracks clacking below our feet as we rolled east across Indiana. "*Secession* means the Southerners are breaking away, or seceding, from our present Union of thirty-three states to form their own confederacy of sorts."

"Thirty-four," I corrected, still feeling a little snippy since our argument about her leaving me behind. "Kansas announced statehood last month."

I turned that word *secession* around on my tongue for a while, then tossed the pin aside and picked up my *Chicago Press & Tribune*. The papers were full of stories about these Southern "fire-eaters," as they called themselves. From what I understood, these rebels wanted to put Mr. Lincoln in a grave before he could even recite the oath of office.

"There is talk of bloodshed in the news," I said. "They're saying the South will take up guns against the North in war—they're threatening to kill Mr. Lincoln himself."

"So I've heard," Aunt Kitty said, her voice tight. She turned her gaze out the window, watching the colorless winter landscape roll by.

I tried to offer a more cheerful bit of news.

"Listen to this, Aunt Kitty. Mr. Lincoln has taken off by train from Illinois just like us. Only he's heading for the White House in Washington," I said, peering up from the newspaper. "Perhaps our paths will intersect, and we'll get to see how tall the man is in real life."

Aunt Kitty told me to put the newspaper down and get ready. But I wanted to know why we were bothering with a trek to Baltimore, Maryland, for some ordinary old case when we really needed to be in South Carolina or Mississippi, where treason was happening on a grand scale.

"Pay attention," Aunt Kitty said peevishly, tugging the newspaper from my hands and setting it on the bench beside me. "We need to prepare for what's ahead—Baltimore is a hotbed. Mr. Pinkerton's detective agency has been hired to keep tabs on the railroad lines in and out of Baltimore, and any plans to destroy them. But I suspect there is something more evil in the wind. I will not say more on it, but know that Baltimore aligns itself with the South. It is full of angry men and women ready to die for their cause and their way of life. If we are found out, Nell, it could turn quite ugly."

Aunt Kitty was no dramatist, so when she got worked up, I knew I should be on guard. I sat up a little straighter and listened closely as she went on.

"Our steps cannot falter. We cannot fail in this mission—*cannot*. Now hear me well. While I did not want to bring you on such a dangerous mission, you can be of help to me on this case after all, Nell. We shall pose as Southern sisters this time, hailing from Montgomery, Alabama. I am Mrs. Barley, and you are my sister, Miss Matilda Maddox. I believe that with those ears of yours, you can listen for any dark plans as well as I can."

"Matilda?" I protested. "What kind of name is Matilda? Makes me sound bulky."

Aunt Kitty snapped up the newspaper and whacked me on the shoulder with it. "Enough childishness, Nell! I don't have time for it. Now I'll need you to change into your disguise at the next stop this train makes, while I meet with Mr. Pinkerton and the other detectives in the adjoining railcar. I expect you to look sharp upon my return!"

And she marched off in such a dander, I imagined smoke trailing behind her.

I leaned back on the bench in the rattling car, alone and shivering. The trees through the window were spindly and bare, and a thin layer of snow whitened the landscape as far as my eye could see. There was an etching of frost forming along the corner of the window, the glass doing little to keep the bitter fingers of winter from finding their way inside our railcar. I couldn't help but feel the whole country was in the grip of the same chill.

Was the United States tearing apart, just as Mr. Lincoln had warned about a house divided? I picked up the blue cockade again and turned it in my fingers, shuddering to think of what Jemma would do if she saw me mixing among Baltimore's secessionists. But it seemed we were going undercover right into the hornet's nest itself. Perhaps Jemma might be proud to know we were spying on the haters of freedom.

As Aunt Kitty had directed, at the first stop I left

the train and donned the costume she'd packed in my
bag—a gorgeous gown of deep green taffeta and black
lace that I'd seen at the Pinkerton office with Mr. Bangs
so many months ago. It fit me perfectly, sullied only by
the despicable blue cockade I pinned to my breast. I
twisted my hair into a low knot, then carefully climbed
back aboard the train and stepped down the aisle.

A familiar voice, deep and gravelly, interrupted my
thoughts.

"Good afternoon, young lady. Delightful weather
we're having for February, wouldn't you say?"

The playful Detective Webster was standing before
me, only this time he was clean-shaven and in a new
winter suit. I braced for one of his jokes, but he seemed
earnest. I turned to look behind me to see who the
"young lady" might be—perhaps another rider my age?
But there was no one else in the long aisle of the railcar
but me.

"Pleased to make your acquaintance," he continued
formally, taking my green-gloved hand in his and bowing like a real gentleman until his head nearly touched
my knuckle.

I yanked my hand from his and immediately jabbed at his rib cage with an affectionate but firm punch.

Detective Webster jumped back as if I'd poked him with a hot stick.

"I beg pardon, miss!"

"Do you not know me, Mr. Webster?" I asked, unsure whether he was making me the butt of his joke. He was always teasing, but this time his voice sounded sincere.

"Jiminy Christmas! Nell Warne?" he whispered, his expression confounded. I could swear I saw a blush spreading like wildfire from out of his starched collar, up his neck, and engulfing his cheeks. "It cannot be. I took you for . . . for a . . . for a lady!"

Chapter 33

In Which Aunt Kitty Worms Out Secrets, and I Prove to Be a Belle of the Ball

M iss Matilda Maddox, you are the wittiest, most fascinating flower to bloom in Baltimore in years."

Good gravy! If what I was dishing out was considered witty, then these dunderheads must spend all their live-long days under a rock.

Nevertheless, I batted my eyes and waved my dainty black fan at my four companions, trying hard to appear like I was enjoying their company. I shot a look over at Aunt Kitty in her flouncy blue gown, laughing and talking at the center of her own circle of wild-eyed

Southern hospitality. I knew we were Mr. Pinkerton's only detectives at the Barnum Hotel tonight. I'd overheard Aunt Kitty say Hattie Lawton and Detective Webster had already slipped off to the town of Perrymansville not far from here, where they were to pass themselves off as husband and wife and learn what secrets they could.

While the Barnum Hotel was teeming with life, I was enjoying it with a particularly noisy quartet of rabble-rousers. They surrounded me in chairs and on their knees, and as I scanned their young faces, I figured their ages were about sixteen. And they must have taken me for thereabouts, too, though I was only thirteen, give or take.

Beneath the miles and miles of petticoats I was wearing to fill out my shiny green skirt, I shuffled my boots and tried to get comfortable on the stiff sofa. But it was no use, as one of the dim boys pressed in a little closer and crushed my gown under his knee.

I batted my eyes and tried to make sense of their blustery, boastful talk.

"That devil Lincoln is soon to be riding the train through Baltimore," began the baby-faced rogue who was kneeling on my costume.

"On his way to Washington, yes," continued the second, shouting over his companion for a chance to sound brave, "but he won't leave Baltimore alive!"

And not to be outdone, the third and fourth cohorts raised their voices and their fists, vowing, "The abolitionist traitor will never take the oath of office, not if there's a Son of the South alive to stop him!"

I'd read enough newspapers by now to know about abolitionists, and I did not think the term deserved to go hand in hand with the word *traitor*. I fanned my face a little faster and resisted the urge to smack these blithering cretins roundly on their hot heads.

I listened keenly to their brave talk, but my attention was distracted by a lively table just a few quick steps away. Seated at their party were two men—both handsome with heads of wavy black hair and well-shaped mustaches—who appeared alarmingly familiar to me.

I knew those faces, but how? And what if they recognized me? Would they call out, "Penelope Potter, we meet again"? Or holler, "Ali, the fortune-teller's assistant"? Or "Miss Charity Englehart, what a pleasure"? I held my fan steady before my cheeks and peered over it as my four secessionist simpletons continued puffing their chests like a bunch of barnyard roosters.

Suddenly the two mustached men rose from their table and, leaving their dining companions behind, began walking toward our group with great purpose. I couldn't help but gasp and lower my eyes, shielding my identity beneath the brim of my black bonnet, which Aunt Kitty had be-feathered with practically an entire bird.

"Good to see you again, sirs," yelped the rebel to my right, now leaping to his feet and grinding my beautiful skirt beneath his manure-encrusted boot. He was vigorously shaking the hands of the two familiar men as if they were old friends, then he began boister- ously introducing the members of our party. When he at last came to me, I could feel my heart pounding in my throat for fear that my identity was about to be revealed.

Our entire operation seemed doomed as I rose to my feet.

"Miss Matilda Maddox," the baby-faced rebel was saying, his cheeks growing splotchy-red from excite- ment, "I'd like to introduce you to Mr. Edwin Booth and his brother John Wilkes Booth. They are among our most talented theater actors here in Baltimore. If you were to read the newspapers, Miss Matilda, you would know all about them."

I wanted nothing more than to stomp on his toes with my own heavy boot and call him an illiterate oaf. I'd probably read more newspapers in one week than he'd read in his entire lifetime! But instead I fanned myself and gave a friendly curtsy, nearly overcome with relief that the strangers and I were not acquainted. I merely knew them from the theater posters around town.

"We were just investigating the music we're hearing," said one of the Booth brothers, twisting the end of his mustache. "There seems to be dancing in the grand ballroom."

And before I could say Yankee Doodle, I was swept onto the marble dance floor and forced to divide my time among four of the South's clumsiest, rock-footed mutineers.

"I believe I have had quite enough of rebels," I announced a few hours later, once Aunt Kitty and I finally retired to our room upstairs. I threw myself onto the bed and freed my sweaty feet from the brown boots. "When they weren't talking about stopping Abe Lincoln from becoming president, they were going on and on about the barber at the hotel. They said a Northerner shouldn't get too close to his shaving blade.

"The way they talked, you'd think the two were linked somehow. Is it possible Mr. Lincoln is due for a shave when he passes through Baltimore?"

Aunt Kitty paced the room trying to make sense of what we picked up from our Southern companions. While she must have been tuckered out from pretending to be Mrs. Barley and insinuating herself into the highest levels of Southern society, she didn't show it.

"Ferr-*ini*, Ferr-*ani*, Ferr-*adoni*," she muttered. "I could not catch the pronunciation. I believe that is the barber you heard about, too. The name sounded from Italy or Corsica, I believe."

"The brutes I was with called him Ferrandini. Do you think he knows how to make that Italian dish we ate in Mississippi?" I hollered, hopping up from the bed in my bare feet and ready to go call on this suspicious barber. *"Macaroni a l'Italienne with Fromage.* The most wonderful dish I ever tasted!"

Aunt Kitty stopped her pacing and glared at me. I got the hint and hopped back onto the bed, taking a bite out of a bright red apple from the bedside bowl.

"I believe you've got it right, Nell. This suspicious barber is someone Mr. Pinkerton needs to visit. We must get a telegraph off as quickly as possible."

Aunt Kitty's pen moved furiously across the page as she perched at a desk near the foot of our beds. I quickly escaped my gown and corset and propped my overworked feet on the pillow to air them out. I shifted gingerly on the bed, my back stiff from bearing the weight of all those petticoats—perhaps wearing ten was too many.

"I believe I know when it will happen," Aunt Kitty said quietly as she dipped her pen into the inkwell. "And we know who is involved. The way things are shaping up, Nell, it's much more than the railroads that need protecting now."

I listened to the scratch of the pen's nib and burned with curiosity. *When it will happen?* What did Aunt

Kitty mean by that? What was she telling Mr. Pinkerton? I could peek at the page, but I knew Aunt Kitty did the same thing as me and Jemma. She wrote her messages to Mr. Pinkerton in code. I stole a quick glance at her paper, the loopy cursive writing as neat and tidy as her hair.

"Nuts to Philadelphia and Harrisburg," she wrote.

I took another noisy bite of my apple and mulled this over. We were risking our skins in this hornet's nest for some nuts?

What did that message mean? Jemma could figure it out. If only she were here to read it with me. I pulled out my cigar box and sifted through it until I came across Jemma's most recent letter, sent at Christmastime.

Chapter 34

<hr/>

In Which Jemma Gives Me Clues to Find the Maple Tree

December 17, 1860

Dear Nell,

Does it snow there? We had a blizzard last night that will keep us locked inside until Christmas. I don't know what I'll do to keep the little ones happy. All they want to do is play blindman's buff and ghost-in-the-graveyard, but that's hard to do inside our tiny house.

I can hardly get a moment to myself these days, so I'm tucked under a blanket trying to write to you by moonlight. I'll make it fast, lest Mama or the little ones catch me and start to holler.

Mama told me something the other night once the babies were asleep, and I need to tell it to you quick. She said the Pickled Onion didn't know about the Underground Railroad back when she lived there, and neither did her husband. It was secret, even though our families were friends. I believe the Maple Tree is the only one who could explain about it, if only you could see him.

I know sometimes the Pickled Onion takes you traveling with her. If you get to visiting Phil O'Dell again, call on the Maple Tree. Mama doesn't know it, but I've been told where to find him. He lives at the corner where two streets meet. One street is a number—the age your brother was when he died of scarlet fever. The other is something I used to put in your hair to scare you.

No matter who else might be reading our letters, you're the only one who can figure out this cipher. Just use that smart head of yours.

> Your friend forever and ever,
> Jemma

Chapter 35

In Which Aunt Kitty Takes Us to Another City, and I Take Off to Find the Maple Tree

Our days in Baltimore were busy with socializing and eavesdropping, not to mention dressing up in our fine gowns. But before long Aunt Kitty whisked us off to the nearest train depot and we boarded a locomotive for New York City.

"I hear the theater shows there are grand," I said with a cool voice, trying not to reveal my excitement of exploring a big city. "I've saved up a bit of money for adventuring. Perhaps we could attend a comedy, to lift the spirits?"

Aunt Kitty said this was no time for make-believe

when we had such a dangerous case unfolding before us. That kept me on the edge of my seat the whole ride north to New York. Did this have anything to do with "Nuts," as Aunt Kitty had written? Or with the razor-wielding barber in the Baltimore hotel? Had that barber moved to New York? Was that city full of angry secessionists, too? But how, when it wasn't a Southern state?

I had too many questions swirling in my head to ask my aunt, knowing how short on patience she was with me most days. I tried to figure things out on my own, paying close attention as Aunt Kitty kept appointments with important-looking businessmen at all hours of the day and night, their conversations hushed and tense. She passed them letters. They passed her ones right back. There was a lot of whispering and telegraphing and general secretiveness, the details of which even my sensitive ears could not take in.

"You're a strange woman, Mrs. Barley," one of them told Aunt Kitty in frustration one morning. He wanted her to disclose more information, so I leaned my body closer toward their chairs at the window in the hopes of overhearing some nugget that would help me make sense of this latest case. But Aunt Kitty refused to divulge any of Mr. Pinkerton's secrets.

Once we retired to our hotel room, Aunt Kitty rushed to her pen and paper and began secretively writing a new message. I peered over her shoulder.

"Plums, the operation is heating up in Baltimore," she wrote, quickly dipping her pen into the blue-black ink, and I wondered who Plums was.

Mr. Pinkerton?

When she spied me behind her, I made a point to unfurl my newspaper with a noisy flip of my wrists and head for the fireplace to read. I was caught up with the real news of the day—Mr. Lincoln's journey across the countryside into Washington. The newspaper said he would raise the flag over Independence Hall this week in Philadelphia, then journey on to the Pennsylvania capitol in Harrisburg. Those were to be his final stops before making his way down to Baltimore and on to the White House in Washington. The paper even printed his train schedule.

Wait a minute, Harrisburg and Philadelphia?

Those were the cities Aunt Kitty had mentioned in one of her earlier messages. And Baltimore? We'd spent a good long while in that cesspool.

"Our work here in New York is completed, Matilda," Aunt Kitty announced abruptly the next afternoon. I was seated in the hotel restaurant, just about to sink my teeth into a buttery roasted goose. "We've met with the gentlemen Mr. Pinkerton wanted us to meet. The information we needed is obtained—I won't tell you more on that. Now grab your bag and get moving. We've got to catch the next train to Philadelphia."

We were heading to Philadelphia? Thoughts began swirling in my mind like fireflies in a mason jar. I'd read about Philadelphia in Jemma's letter.

I got up from the table in a hurry, straightening my bonnet and grabbing my black knit bag. Maybe I was getting used to being a detective's assistant and always on the move, because I didn't even bother waiting around for the hotel dessert—and it would have been my first time to taste iced cream.

Just about an hour later, with our railcar rocking gently from side to side, we rolled south from New York toward the city of Philadelphia. I pulled out my cigar box and riffled through its contents to find Jemma's Christmas letter. Unfolding the pages, I ignored my aunt's roving eye and read openly. With our secret code, Jemma's letter would make about as much sense to Aunt Kitty as her telegraphs were making to me.

"I have too much to do in Philadelphia to keep my eyes on you, Matilda," she announced quietly, darting looks at passengers around us to make sure nobody was listening. "So I want you to stay put at the train station until I call for you."

"Please don't make me sit still," I began, making sure to keep from whining. Aunt Kitty could handle an argument, but the second a tinge of fussiness colored my voice, she went deaf. "I didn't get to see any of New York City. And it's not healthy to stay cooped up inside. Please allow me to meander a bit and explore the sites. Philadelphia is a city rich in historical significance."

For a beat or two, Aunt Kitty squinted at me with a look of doubt. I think she was trying to measure if I really had a lick of interest in sites of *historical significance* or if I was sassing her. Thankfully she did not have the time or patience to talk it through.

"Here are a few dimes. If the circumstances were different, I wouldn't allow a girl your age to wander off," she said, sizing me up with a long stare. "Make sure you stay fed and stay safe. I want you back at the train station on time, not a minute late. Do you understand?"

I promised up and down that I'd buy a proper meal and not wander off too far. And I had to cross my heart that I'd be back on time if she'd just let me scoot out of her clutches for a few hours of freedom. She seemed happy to be rid of me, and once the train finally stopped moving, she threw me a quick nod and marched out the depot doors to take care of her detective work.

She would never guess that I was doing my own.

I sat down on a bench in the depot and ran my finger over the most important part of Jemma's last letter.

> He lives at the corner where two streets meet. One street is a number—the age your brother was when he died of scarlet fever. The other is something I used to put in your hair to scare you.

The first clue was easy to figure out. My brother Jeremiah died of the fever when he was seventeen. But as to figuring out the other street, well, there was a long list of things Jemma and I did as girls to scare each other.

I slipped the letter back into my black bag and left the train station, crossing the busy road. The sign read Broad Street, so I followed it north into the city. Nobody seemed to care that I was a lady on my own, and I kept my smile to myself so as not to draw unwanted attention. It felt good to be free and adventuring alone. I stopped by a general store and picked up two sassafras candy sticks for a penny to help me concentrate on Jemma's second clue.

"Daisy chains, pine needles, mud," I mumbled to myself. Those were all things we put into each other's hair now and again. But to scare me?

I fumbled for some coins to pay a newspaper boy. When I asked him to direct me toward Seventeenth Street, he shoved a *Public Ledger* at me and pointed west with a gruff bark. "Take a left turn at any of the next streets, lady."

Tucking the newspaper into my bag, I glanced at the name on the nearest street sign. Pine Street, it read.

"Ah-ha!" I shouted. "Seventeenth and Pine Streets! This must be where Jemma's daddy lives!" I walked to the corner, but something didn't add up. I watched a horse *clip-clop* up the street, pulling a long wagon loaded with sacks of flour and other dry goods. There were no houses around here, just shops and businesses. And come to think of it, Jemma might have put pine needles in my hair, but that would hardly scare me. I decided to walk on, passing two more streets—Cypress and Spruce.

I was about to lose hope amid all these tree names when a stranger told me the name of the next one. Locust Street. And that's when it hit me.

"Grasshoppers!" I shouted, drawing strange looks from a few passersby.

Chapter 36

In Which I Discover the Maple
Tree and a Few Truths About
Chemung County

The memories suddenly came rushing back to me: Jemma used to put grasshoppers in my hair to frighten me, and I liked to put June bugs on her shoulders to give her a shock.

A little chill of excitement ran through me as I realized how good Jemma's clues had been. I marched along the dirt boulevard, the weather bright and sunny despite the February cold. I skipped over a puddle as I hustled past homes painted bright white or yellow. They had wide wooden porches and pointy roofs.

There were one or two stone mansions tucked behind thick shrubs and wrought-iron fences.

Finally I reached the corner of Seventeenth and Locust Streets. Staring up at a gray stone house with a wide black door in the middle of it, I was breathless—more from nerves and a tight corset than actual exertion. I saw someone moving across the yard with a rake, tending to the broken twigs and dead leaves. But otherwise the house was silent.

Now that I was here, I had no earthly idea what I was going to do. I couldn't just saunter up to the door of these refined Philadelphians and ask to have tea with the Maple Tree. What was I thinking? I began to pace back and forth, turning ideas around in my mind.

"You've grown into a real lady, Miss Cornelia," came a deep voice. I turned, peering over a spindly shrub, and found myself gazing into the gentle face of Jemma's father, Old Joseph Tuthill. He was a solid man, just half a head taller than I was, though I remembered him being as big as a tree—a maple tree. Sturdy and strong, that was Old Joseph. His hair was white with age, but his face was the same as when I knew him back in my days with Jemma in Chemung

County. "You've got your father's eyes and mouth, that's for certain, but you're a real lady."

I caught my breath, searching for where to begin.

"That's kind of you to say, Mr. Tuthill," I stammered, my joy at seeing him nearly leaving me speechless. "I wish I could see how Jemma grew up. I bet she's a real lady now, too."

He nodded sadly and hesitated for a moment, and I wished I could scoop the air around me and pull those words back into my mouth. It probably pained him to think about Jemma and the rest of his family. Jemma said she hadn't seen her daddy for years.

He pointed over toward a cluster of fir trees on the far side of the yard, where we could speak more privately. A few ladies pushing baby prams passed us, and Mr. Tuthill tipped his hat to each of them in a friendly manner. His eyes seemed to take in everything around us, and the thought struck me that as a conductor on the Underground Railroad here, he was probably a good detective, too.

"I got word from Saint Catharines about you coming. I hear you're wantin' to know about your daddy and his brother, Mr. Matthew," he said, running his fingers through his trim gray beard. "I'm real sorry for your loss."

I nodded, unsure of whether my voice had left me. I noticed Old Joseph's hands were calloused and scarred, as knobby as tree bark. "Miss Cornelia, your daddy was my friend, and what happened to his brother Matthew that night was a tragedy. I'll never forget it. Drove his widow right out of town, as I recall."

"That's right," I said. "She's my aunt Kitty. I'm trying hard to set things right with her. But she'll need more than my word about what happened, Mr. Tuthill. She'll need evidence."

He nodded some more and stared into my face like his mind was falling back through time, and I suspect it was. I felt my cheeks flush with embarrassment—it suddenly felt reckless being here with Old Joseph, stirring up the ashes of my family's past. Why didn't I just let it die out? Why was I chasing down ghosts like this?

"When I heard Matthew Warne on his horse that night, we were in the woods a good ways off from the farms. Jemma's mama was at the front with the babies.

Jemma was with me at the back. She was sad to leave you, her best friend, that was for sure."

I didn't speak, the pictures of that night coming to life in my mind like I was there, too, instead of tucked safely away in my bed and sleeping.

"Your daddy, Cornelius, was out in front, leading us to the river. The babies were crying, they were so tired and out of sorts—it was long past midnight, and we'd been walking along a dried-up creek bed for a few hours already. That's when a man came riding up toward us—we could almost feel the hoofbeats. There had been slave hunters thereabouts, so every one of us was shaking with fear. This man on horseback, he must have heard us, heard one of the babies crying. And he came riding up, and he called for us to stop. But nothing was stopping your daddy."

Old Joseph paused and scratched his beard before going on.

"There was no moon that night. Sometimes I think if there had been, maybe Cornelius Warne would have recognized his own brother. But he didn't. And in the rush of panic that swept over all of us, your daddy fired his gun."

I swallowed hard, but my mouth was as dry as cotton.

"We ran as fast as we could, but a bloodhound caught our trail and started barking. Right away Jemma knew that hound dog. And she raced ahead to catch up with your daddy. 'That's Matthew Warne's dog, Mr. Cornelius,' she told him. And that's when we knew something terrible had just happened. We were so far from home, we pushed on to the river, where a conductor was waiting with a skiff. I helped Jemma and the babies get in. I kissed Jemma's mama good-bye. Then I sent them to follow the Drinking Gourd. That North Star would have to lead them on to Canada without me.

"I was torn. But I couldn't leave your daddy like that, knowing his own brother might be lying dead back behind us in the woods. We'd grown up together, our families."

We were silent for few moments. Then he reached one of his knobby brown hands into his coat and felt around over his heart. He produced a small picture frame no bigger than his palm. It was a deep crimson with gold trim, and a swirly gold inlay framed the image.

I leaned in close. My breath could have steamed the delicate glass case. It was a daguerreotype of a man and a woman. It was probably their wedding day, I assumed, judging by the bride's veil and gown— simple though they were. Her eyes were intense, staring so fiercely up at me from the copperplate that I recognized her right away.

"Aunt Kitty," I whispered. Then my gaze shifted to the groom. "And Uncle Matthew. I couldn't recall his face. But seeing him here—it all comes back to me now."

I had a sudden recollection of booming laughter and the thick smell of pipe tobacco. I remembered teasing and mischief and strong arms swinging me into the air. Uncle Matthew was like Detective Webster in his joking and boundless sense of joy.

"I held on to it to give to his widow. After I got word from Saint Catharines, I've been holding it for you," Old Joseph said, his voice growing more urgent. "You take it to Kitty, now. You tell her it was an accident what happened to her Matthew. He'd gotten wind of Cornelius helping my family escape to freedom, just as some slave hunters showed up back in town. Matthew was riding out to warn us when he died. He was doing something brave, Matthew was.

"And Cornelius, he didn't mean what happened. I saw it myself. Cornelius Warne lived the rest of his days in despair over shooting Matthew. That's why the drinking and gambling got worse. That's why he left your mama, your brothers, and you to fend for your-selves on the farm."

I couldn't speak for the knot that had tied itself around my heart. I kept staring at the image of Aunt Kitty as a bride, so soft and sweet-looking. The only picture she'd ever sat for in her life. I thought about her and Matthew.

"And my daddy?"

"He did good, too, your daddy," Old Joseph contin-ued. "I want you to remember that, now, you hear me? Cornelius Warne could never forget what happened to his brother. And neither could I. So that's why we both carried on."

And I knew exactly what he meant by that—*carried on.*

Jemma's daddy was in Philadelphia helping slaves find their way to freedom. That's why he didn't live with Jemma and her mama and the rest of the family in Canada. He couldn't—not with the ghosts of Matthew Warne and his own brother Ezekiel haunting his mind all these years. And my daddy had been haunted, too.

"But what about him?" I asked Old Joseph, my voice husky with sadness. "How did Cornelius die?"

Old Joseph shook his head, his eyes searching my face in confusion.

"I thought you knew, Miss Cornelia. Those same slave catchers came back again and again." He paused for a long time, then he closed his eyes.

"They weren't just after slaves that time. His body washed up in the Chemung River."

I felt a sob catch in my throat, but I trapped it just in time. I took a deep breath and closed my eyes, wiggling my feet in those heavy boots. And suddenly I understood what it meant to have faith in someone. Faith wasn't about evidence and eyewitnesses, like with Aunt Kitty and Mr. Pinkerton's other detectives. Faith was something you knew inside—from your heart all the way to the tips of your toes.

"Jemma will, too, you know," I said gently. "Carry on, that is. She wanted me to tell you that she's coming to join you, Mr. Tuthill. I don't know when or how. But Jemma means to carry on, too. And I believe she will."

I reached up my hand, intending to tuck the delicate gold frame under my bonnet, but I stopped myself. This was too important. Jemma's daddy was looking at me with those wise old eyes, and I felt the weight of all the years and all the ghosts. I pulled a linen hankie from my sleeve and gently wrapped the delicate frame in it. Then I slipped it into the pocket of my flowing green skirt. And I knew I wouldn't be able to let go until I reached Aunt Kitty.

Chapter 37

In Which Aunt Kitty Proves Exasperating, and I Prove My Case

unt Kitty," I hollered when I saw her across the wide waiting area of the Philadelphia train depot. "Aunt Kitty, you won't believe what I've got to show you!"

Night had fallen, and even by the yellow glow of the gaslights, I could see her irritation flare up. She turned from her conversation with a pale, nervous-looking man and shot me a look that stopped me in my tracks.

"Excuse me, young lady," she said coolly. "My name is Mrs. Barley. I think you are confused."

And turning her back on me, she and the pasty man

walked off toward the ticket counter. I fought the urge to remove one of my boots and throw it at the back of her head. She was infuriating in her stubborn dedication to work. And frankly, sometimes her job seemed silly—like a costume party with a bunch of ridiculous grown-ups.

I stood there in the pale circle of light shaking with anger. And I didn't know which enraged me more—that there was never a good time to talk about what happened to my daddy and her Matthew, or that I had done it again and given away her true identity.

I skulked over to a nearby bench and sat down, letting out a deep sigh that echoed in the vast waiting area. After a while, I watched Aunt Kitty cross the marble floor toward me. She was her usual calm self, her spine as straight as a fence post and her gait regal like Queen Victoria. I noticed more than a few heads turn to watch her pass. The cavernous train depot amplified every sound, and I heard the *swish-swish* of her full blue skirts as she approached.

"I have secured four double berths in the sleeping car of the ten-fifty train bound for Washington," she whispered tensely. And then, seeing my frantic search for which train she was talking about, she pointed her gaze toward the right one and went on. "The sleeping car is the very last. The rear door will remain unlocked, as I am awaiting the arrival of my poor, sick brother who cannot walk without aid."

"I didn't know you had a sick brother..." I began. But then I snapped back, realizing Aunt Kitty was still in character for the latest case. My cheeks burned red with embarrassment.

"Why are you so distracted, Matilda?" she hissed, looking around to see if we were overheard. "Have you no sense? Have you no understanding of the gravity of the situation?"

I jumped to my feet and discovered that I'd grown these past many months—I was almost her same height. Despite the slight difference, I still looked her straight in the eye.

"Of course I don't know the gravity of the situation," I said testily, "because you don't trust me enough to tell me what's going on."

Aunt Kitty glanced over my shoulder, and I suddenly became aware of how far my voice must have traveled despite my speaking through a clenched jaw.

All around us, like crows perched on telegraph lines, sat eager observers, their eyebrows raised and their heads cocked to the side as if to hear us better.

"Sit back down immediately, and wait five minutes," Aunt Kitty directed, her voice deadly. "Then proceed to the sleeping car and enter it through the rear door. We can talk privately there without bringing this entire case to rubble on our heads here in the open."

I'd been waiting so long to redeem my daddy, what was another five minutes? But I only lasted about three and a half. That's because a greasy-looking man plunked himself down on the bench beside me, revealing a row of brown teeth when he smiled.

"How do?" he said with a tip of his dirty hat. "Would you like company?"

Quick as lightning, I headed for the heavy front doors as if I were returning to the Philadelphia streets. Then, at the last minute, I dove behind a chalk signboard advertising train tickets to Cincinnati. Crouched down low and counting out a full one hundred and twenty seconds, I finally dashed across the tracks and down the other side of the train all the way to the sleeping car at the very end.

I was breathless when I bounded inside and flung myself into the seat across from Aunt Kitty.

"Foolish child!" she said bitterly. "I thought you had more sense after all this time. But you've proven to me you do not. Such recklessness using my name! On a case of this importance! You irresponsible girl!"

"Stop calling me that," I said in a steely voice I'd picked up from her.

"Calling you what?"

"Girl," I said flatly. "I am not a little girl anymore. I'm thirteen—or thereabouts."

She stared at me with a look of curiosity mixed with rage.

"And I don't want to hear you blather on about another case, Aunt Kitty—all right, *Aunt Kate*! But it's time you do the listening to me for a change. No interruptions."

She turned her eyes away, gazing out the railcar window at the doors that led from the street into the depot. She seemed to be deciding whether she had the patience for me or not.

"It's about my daddy," I began. "And you need to hear me out. He was a good man, just like I've said all along. And just as your beloved Mr. Pinkerton helps the Underground Railroad, my daddy did, too."

Aunt Kate gasped like I'd uttered a blasphemy.

"How dare you speak Mr. Pinkerton's name together in the same breath with your father's," she snapped. "You sound like a child who's been raised on fairy tales. You want to believe that your good-for-nothing father was decent in some way. But he was not. And after all this time witnessing detective work, it seems you haven't learned anything. Where's your proof? Where's your evidence?"

I hesitated for a few seconds, almost losing my nerve. I had no idea how she would handle this moment. I stared into her stern face, the fingers of my left hand turning the picture frame around and around in my skirt pocket.

Finally I pulled out the white hankie and unfolded it, silently holding the delicate gold frame out to her.

Aunt Kate's sharp eyes darted to the picture, but her hands lay useless in her lap. She seemed thunderstruck by what she saw, drawn to the image yet unable to touch it.

"How?" was all she managed.

We sat across from each other in the railcar, and I told her everything I'd learned from Old Joseph Tuthill and from Jemma's letters. We talked about Matthew and what happened the night he died. Some of it she agreed with, some she did not. But as time passed and she finally took the daguerreotype delicately in her hands, I could see my aunt's expression transform. She softened somehow, her eyes squinting just a hint less and her shoulders seeming to slacken. She let out a deep sigh, and I swear I could see the anger of so many years swirl into the air above us like a mist and drift away down the narrow aisle of our railcar.

Finally, she spoke, and her voice sounded distant, like it was coming from miles away.

"He carried this picture with him everywhere he went, Matthew did."

I nodded silently that I understood. I always did like the idea of carrying a little piece of somebody with me, whether it was a memory or a photograph.

Or a pair of scraped-up boots.

"Old Joseph helped dig Matthew's grave," I whispered. "He said you didn't even come to the funeral."

"I couldn't bear the loss," Aunt Kate finally said. "I didn't know how I could go on, how I'd live without him. I think blaming your daddy was the only way I survived—if I didn't have that anger to hold on to, I would have drowned in the sorrow."

I knew that same sadness. After Mama died, followed so fast by my two brothers, I was heavy with grief. And then when I learned my daddy was gone, too, I slipped into a dark, churning river with no foothold. I felt like I couldn't come up for air from the hopelessness of it all.

"Your father, Nell," Aunt Kate said haltingly. "Tell me what happened to Cornelius in the end."

I took my time, partly because I wanted to get it right. But also because my heart was up high in my throat, making it hard to get the words out. I told her what Jemma had explained in her letters and what Old Joseph had told me this very afternoon.

"Since it was too dangerous for Old Joseph to stay in Chemung County after Matthew's death, and with his family having gotten away to Canada, he came down here where he could help. He sent free blacks and runaway slaves north toward my daddy. And my daddy helped get them on to Saint Catharines in Canada," I explained.

"The way Old Joseph said, what happened with my daddy was a lot like the night your Matthew died a few years before. My daddy was leading a band of folks through the woods toward the Chemung River, just like he did for Jemma and her family, when he heard someone following him in the woods. But this time it wasn't your Matthew and his bloodhound trailing behind him. This time it really was a slave hunter—four of them, Old Joseph said. They shot him dead and threw his body in the water."

Aunt Kate's face was stony and her lips tight, but there was something tender in her eyes. And I knew she was sorry for the bad things she had said about my daddy all this time. But I didn't need to hear her apologize. I pulled out my cigar box from the bottom of my bag and unfolded a worn paper—my vocabulary list. Lots of the words were marked off by now, she'd been torturing me with them for so long. My eyes raced down the page to the last bunch, and I picked out the one I was looking for. It read *redemption*.

"I think I know what this means, Aunt Kate," I said

softly, taking a quick glance into her eyes. They were just a little watery, but it could have been the cold night.

"I am impressed, Nell. You make a good detective."

And just like that, my eyes were wet, too. Only before I knew what was happening, the tears were pouring down my cheeks and I was bawling like a bald-headed baby. Aunt Kate scooted across to sit next to me, whispering *shush* over and over again. I quickly quieted down—it was not a good idea to go blowing our cover all over again.

"You really think I'm a detective?" I sniffled, trying to control another sob as it fought to get out of my chest. "Just like you?"

"I do," she said, and she tenderly patted my hand. I felt her warm breath on my cheek and smelled that familiar scent of licorice. "Though you seem to be baffled by the clues to our current case, Nell, and that surprises me. Perhaps you were too distracted tracking down your daddy's story to pay close attention to this one."

I sat up straight and faced her square. "I do know what this one's about, Aunt Kate. I have to admit I peeked over your shoulder at your messages."

She scowled. But we both knew that peeking over people's shoulders was all in a day's work for a good detective.

"I know the code name is Nuts. I suspect it is a man. And I believe he's coming here to Philadelphia on his way to Baltimore. I imagine he could be a wealthy peanut farmer who is being threatened by his wife's lover. Perhaps we're to protect him from robbery? Poison? No, maybe it's—"

But there was no more time for pleasant conversation as Aunt Kate sprang to her feet, nearly sending me tumbling to the floor of the railcar. And craning my neck to see what she spied out the window, I heard her utter only one word.

"Assassination."

Chapter 38

In Which Aunt Kate Takes the Lead, and I Try to Hurry and Catch Up

The enormous wooden doors at the end of the depot opened, allowing three figures to step inside. I watched them approach the train—Mr. Pinkerton was on the left, but I did not know the two other men. On the right was a nondescript gentleman of middling age, height, and handsomeness. But in the center, leaning on Mr. Pinkerton's arm, was a stooped man hobbling on a wooden cane. A black coat was draped over his shoulders, the arms hanging empty. He wore a dark cloth hat whose wide brim and round top obscured his eyes, which I was trying without success to catch.

"My brother, how I've missed you," Aunt Kate announced dramatically, descending from the train's rear platform and greeting Mr. Pinkerton's party as it reached the sleeping car. A few travelers passed on the right and left, but none seemed to pay attention to our group. "You must be exhausted, dear. Please come lie down."

She ushered them onto the train, right past me, paying close attention to the stooped man. The four of them immediately took the berth across the aisle and drew the heavy red curtain for privacy. I heard deep voices as they spoke but could not get the shape of their words.

Within minutes, the wheels began to turn and the train started rolling down the tracks toward Washington. I sat there alone on my bench like a bottle of ginger ale that had been shaken up—so many notions were bubbling in my head, I thought I might explode. When the ticket collector came through, Aunt Kate emerged into the aisle and handed him exactly what he needed, so he didn't even bother to draw back the curtain and peek at the others.

"He is so tall, he cannot even lie straight in his

berth," Aunt Kate whispered, taking her seat across from me with a breathy grin. I knew she was wondering if I'd deciphered the secret, but as always I was still a few steps behind her.

Mr. Pinkerton appeared a short time later, standing in the aisle and leaning low to speak with Aunt Kate in her seat. "I have men positioned all the way down the line from Philadelphia into Baltimore," he said in a deep murmur. "One raised lantern means all's well. And two"—he paused, his eyes flicking to me for a half second—"well, have your revolver ready, Mrs. Warne."

I'd never seen Mr. Pinkerton so tense. I stared at the paisley pattern of the long red curtain across the aisle and considered pulling it back to see for myself who we were protecting behind it.

I watched Mr. Pinkerton step onto the rear platform, I assumed to keep an eye out for the lantern signals. As he tugged the small wooden door shut behind him, stopping the rush of cold night air into the car, I turned back to study my aunt. "No one but Mr. Pinkerton," she said, her eyes never leaving the mystery berth beside us, "shall go in or go out."

And as she repositioned herself on the cushioned bench opposite mine, her gaze locked, I didn't dare speak. I could hardly let myself breathe as I spied, there on her lap, the familiar Colt revolver gleaming in the moonlight, one blue-gloved hand wrapped around the wooden base, the silver barrel glimmering like a night star.

"Aunt Kate," I whispered some time later as the rocking rhythm of the train lulled us not to sleep, but to some tense, contemplative place. "You must tell me everything that's happening. My imagination has gone wild, and I need to know the truth about all this secret service you're up to. What will happen when we reach Baltimore?"

"You have the clues, Nell," she said with an encouraging nod. "I know you can piece this puzzle together on your own."

I sat in still silence, watching the dark scenery rush past. My thoughts were hurtling ahead as well. I worked it out in my mind again and again, but I was too timid to wager a guess—what if Aunt Kate and the others laughed at my wild imagination?

But still, the facts were lined up before me like books on a shelf.

I'd read enough newspapers these past weeks to know that another train was due to be traveling these tracks the next morning. It was the Lincoln Special, ferrying our new president into the nation's capital. Was it possible he was slipping into Washington under the cover of darkness? Stooped and dressed in disguise?

But why?

"He won't leave Baltimore alive."

"The abolitionist traitor will never take the oath of office."

"Assassination."

I turned from the window to stare back at the red curtain. Aunt Kate was still at her post, revolver at the ready.

"It is him, isn't it?" I whispered. "That's Honest Abe we're protecting over there, isn't it? Our own Honest Abe."

Aunt Kate kept her head turned toward the curtain, but the smile that beamed in her eyes told me all I needed to know. I'd done it on my own—I'd solved the mystery. But before she could utter a word of confirmation, a sudden lurch from the train sent me flying from my seat. Such a screech pierced the night, I felt a shiver of fright race up my shoulders. I shuddered as I tried to right myself back on my bench again.

"What's happening?" I asked as the train's shrieking brakes slowed us to a halt. "Why are we stopping?"

Aunt Kate's eyes darted from the heavy red curtain to the back door of the railcar, where Mr. Pinkerton was still standing guard.

"I believe we've reached Baltimore, Nell," Aunt Kate whispered, "the very end of the northern line. The tracks that will take this train into Washington are about one mile away from here. A team of horses must pull our sleeper car through the streets to the Camden Street Station, making us as vulnerable as a newborn babe."

And after a heavy pause, she added, "We will be easy prey to attack."

We watched and waited, for what, I did not know. My blustery secessionist companions? The razor-wielding barber? My heart was thumping in my chest faster than a frightened rabbit's. As we sat in that silent railcar, tense and braced, no one dared to make a sound. I was alone with my imagination, which did not always prove to be a good companion.

Every noise in the night seemed to find its way to my ears. I suddenly wished for my own weapon. Not that I had ever shot a gun at anything that couldn't be put in a pot and served for supper. But then I'd never been forced to. I thought of teaching Aunt Kate how to shoot. What would I do now, if presented with the chance to fire a bullet at a deranged assassin? Would I pull the trigger?

Finally, the wheels began to slowly roll again, and Aunt Kate turned away from the heavy curtain. "I will be returning to the Barnum Hotel to witness the scene throughout the day and to listen for more schemes. Because of the danger, I cannot allow you to come with me into the streets. You must stay on without me, Nell."

It was as if she'd thrown cold water on my face. Aunt Kate was getting off the train here in Baltimore? She was returning to the hornet's nest? What if those fire-eating secessionists found out she was spying on them? What if they knew she wasn't Mrs. Barley at all but a highly skilled detective from Chicago?

I shook my head, preparing to argue. But just as I began to protest, Mr. Pinkerton stepped into the railcar from the back platform and pulled the door shut, slipping his watch into his vest pocket.

"It is three thirty in the morning, and the city of Baltimore—thankfully—appears to be sleeping," he said. "Mrs. Warne, you must be careful as you venture back to the conspirators. I want a full report of the day as it unfolds. Call for a carriage at the ticket window."

Aunt Kate gathered her carpetbag and stood up to go. I saw her slip the revolver into the pocket of her traveling cloak. I jumped to my feet beside her, picking up my feathered bonnet as if to join her.

"But before you take your leave," Mr. Pinkerton continued, "I'd like a brief moment for some formal introductions."

And he finally pulled back that deep-red curtain and moved aside, allowing the mysterious stooped man to step into the aisle. Off came the dark hat to reveal a head of wavy brown hair, thick arched eyebrows, and chiseled cheekbones. He shed his traveling coat, which Aunt Kate took obligingly and folded over her arm. He handed me the walking stick and smiled, only then standing to his full height.

I blinked more than a few times, hardly trusting what my eyes beheld before me. He stood well over six feet tall.

"Mrs. Kate Warne is the chief of my Female Detective Force," Mr. Pinkerton announced to our towering traveling companion. "She has never let me down."

Then, turning to me, he continued, "And this is her able-bodied niece, Miss Nell Warne."

We both gave respectful curtsies, though I couldn't help but add a few bows at the same time, which might have given me the appearance of a whooping crane in courting season.

"There's your Nuts, Nell," my aunt whispered for my ears alone, confirming what I'd spied in her coded messages. I felt a surge of joy mingled with pride pulse through my body as I stood as tall and straight as a lamppost beside her. I quickly ripped the blue cockade off my dress and threw it on the floor behind me.

"Ladies, I'd like to introduce you to Mr. Abraham Lincoln, president-elect of the United States."

My breathing was so fast and my corset so tight,

I could not catch my breath. I shifted my feet in my heavy boots and felt myself swoon. But one sideways look at Aunt Kate, and I knew to collect myself.

"Mrs. Warne, Miss Warne. It is a pleasure to meet you both," he said in a voice that was slightly higher pitched than I'd expected for a man so tall. I noted just the faintest hint of a country twang. "Two detectives together under one roof—I imagine your family must be quite proud."

"It is," my aunt said firmly. "Very proud."

Chapter 39

❧

In Which Aunt Kate Leaves Me

Once we'd made it through the narrow tunnel at Camden Street Station, we had to wait for maintenance work to be completed on the train bound for Washington. This was when Aunt Kate stepped off.

But I could not let her go just like that. I knew she had to leave, to find out more about the assassins' plans. But without me? Quickly I leaped off the rear platform after her. She needed me by her side. What danger was awaiting her in Baltimore? I did not want to imagine what would happen if her true identity were discovered by these bloodthirsty conspirators.

"Why won't you take me with you?" I complained, my words coming out in breathy puffs in the cold night. "I have enough sense to be a help to you, Aunt Kate. Why are you always trying to be rid of me?"

She was doing her fast walking again, approaching a small, redbrick ticket window to inquire about a carriage to the hotel. But she stopped abruptly and turned to face me.

"Let me make something clear to you, Nell Warne. I have eyes that work perfectly well, and I can see that you're not a child anymore. You have been a tremendous help to me since we first came to inherit each other. But I cannot think only of myself and my well-being. I have to think about what's best for you—whether it is Chicago's Home for the Friendless or now, leaving you in the capable hands of Mr. Pinkerton and the others. I don't do it to be rid of you, as you say. I do it because I care for you."

And after a moment's pause, she added, "No matter what your age, I will always want you safe from harm, I will want you happy, and I will want you to keep the company of good people. This is what it means to love someone, Nell."

I'd never heard my aunt use that word—*love*. Not only

did it sound foreign to my ears, it also gave my senses a bit of a shock. That's because it was the last sentiment in the world I was thinking of. Anger, rejection, abandonment. Loneliness. I was familiar with all of those. But *love*? I did not know how to act. My cheeks flared hot with embarrassment, but I hoped the depot's darkness would keep that information from Aunt Kate's detection.

The steam engine let out a puffy hiss on its tracks, reminding us of what lay ahead. I looked into Aunt Kate's face, and there was no trace of the Pickled Onion there. Her expression was gentle and full of caring. She reached over and gave my hand a quick squeeze.

Then she turned and walked away. No more fussing.

As I watched her dark figure disappear into the depot, I opened my mouth to call after her again. But my heart was up so high in my throat, it was hard to speak.

Thoughts were snowflakes swirling in my mind. I couldn't catch one and hold on. I wanted so badly to tell her things. That I loved her, that I worried about her, and most of all, that I wanted to go with her. But the moment was interrupted by something shrill and peculiar piercing the night.

Whistling.

The flesh on my neck and arms went pimply like I'd just climbed out of a cold bath.

It was coming from the far end of the wooden walkway beside the train. Beyond the few gaslights, the night was as black as mud and I could see no figure there. But the sharp melody sliced the cold air around me like a knife. I recognized the Southern tune right away as "Dixie," and the lyrics rushed into my head.

"I wish I was in the land of cotton..."

Immediately I sprang from the ticket area. There was no stopping me as I crossed the wide brick station in seconds. Not another soul was in sight—no conductors, none of the operatives, not even a single passenger. There was just the ghostly melody and me.

Without even thinking, I stepped onto the long wooden walkway and slowly strode toward the whistling. My boots echoed in the darkness with every step.

The whistling grew loud as I approached its source.

"Old times there are not forgotten..."

But my boots were louder.

And they seemed to beat down the "Dixie" tune with every step.

Clip-clomp, clip-clomp.

Then I saw him. More than forty paces ahead, in the small circle of light from the lamppost, a dark figure was standing. He began moving slowly along the walkway, straining to see into the windows of our railcar. Was this the moment we'd been building toward? When the assassin's dagger would plunge into Mr. Lincoln's honorable heart?

I thought again of the rough talk we had heard from the rebel thugs.

"He won't leave Baltimore alive."

"The abolitionist traitor will never take the oath of office."

I would not stop myself—could not stop myself. My mind was too focused. As if propelled by some force beyond even my own power, my boots kept marching down that walkway, louder and stronger and sturdier than I'd ever walked before.

Clip-clomp, clip-clomp.

Pressing close to the train, I made sure the stranger couldn't see me as I stayed just outside each circle of lamplight. I strode faster now, pounding the wooden planks like a drumbeat.

CLIP-CLOMP, CLIP-CLOMP.

His whistling stopped, and the stranger frantically

looked all around him into the darkness. With one last glance in our sleeping car, he turned on his heel and ran. I stopped cold and listened, my heart thudding in my chest, beating out its own rhythm of quiet strength.

Like a rat disappearing into a hole, he was gone, swallowed up by the black night. And the only sound I could hear was his retreating footsteps in the darkness. They faded to a trickle, and then they were gone.

"Hark, who's there?" came a shout, which I knew right away was Mr. Pinkerton.

The steam engine gave another hiss, and the wheels began to roll.

"It's me, Nell Warne," I called. And immediately I saw his hand reach out to me from the rear platform. I grabbed it and leaped, landing squarely on the moving train as it rolled down the tracks bound for Washington and left the menacing city of Baltimore behind.

"Jumping Jehoshaphat, Nell!" boomed Mr. Pinkerton as we picked up speed. "Those boots of yours might have saved the day." And then, as if he reconsidered this thought, he nodded toward the sleeping berth behind us. "And quite possibly more than that!

"Mrs. Warne would be very pleased."

Chapter 40

In Which I Take a Step in a New Direction

We arrived at the great city of Washington just as dawn was turning the sky a rosy gold. Mr. Pinkerton escorted the president-elect through the station and to the waiting arms of his reliable friend. I suspected this was the congressman from Illinois, Elihu Washburne. While I did not recognize his face, I'd read plenty about him in the *Chicago Press & Tribune*. Besides, how many Elihus could there possibly be? There was no welcoming party on the street for Mr. Lincoln this morning, like the ones the newspapers had reported along the entire journey from

Illinois. This morning called for the quiet stealth of a friend's closed carriage and not the booming drums of a marching band.

The inauguration was just days away, and we'd more than done our job of securing the railroad lines into Baltimore. We'd gone even further. We'd delivered Abraham Lincoln safely to Washington and into the history books as the protector of the Union. Mr. Pinkerton stood there on the depot steps like a stone statue, and as we watched Mr. Lincoln climb into the dark carriage, I felt certain that Mr. Pinkerton wasn't ready to give up his secret service to the president.

"I will be busy sending telegraphs all day to the operatives we planted throughout the region," Mr. Pinkerton said, turning to me with a nod, "to Philadelphia and New York. We cut the wires to and from Harrisburg last night when Mr. Lincoln made his hasty departure. But now I'll send word, and the lines will be repaired to working order again."

And he pulled a slip of paper from his breast pocket and tucked it into my hand, saying something about how he wanted me to hold on to it as a keepsake. I wanted to tell him that there was no way a body could forget the night the Pinkerton detectives unraveled the Baltimore plot and saved Abraham Lincoln from an assassin's dagger, even if she lived to be a hundred years old. But instead I just grinned and peeked at the note.

It was one of Mr. Pinkerton's telegraph messages, written in secret code and ready to be sent over the wires to our mother hen Mr. Bangs back at the detective agency in Chicago:

```
G. H. Bang's
80. Washington Street.
Chicago.
Plums has Nuts-arri'd at
Barley-all right.
```

I slipped the paper into my pocket and felt my heart swell. I finally knew all the secrets of this case.

"We'll take the three o'clock train back to Baltimore and meet up with the rest of the operatives at the Barnum Hotel," he said in his Scottish lilt, his tone right back to business as usual. "Mrs. Warne can tell us what the would-be assassins had to say upon discovering that Mr. Lincoln passed safely under their sleeping noses. And we'll find out if they're plotting more treachery against him."

I asked if he thought Aunt Kate might be in much danger today. He warned that all of us were in danger, as the assassins would surely point fingers at whomever they suspected had betrayed them. They would be looking for the spy in their midst.

"Here is your return ticket," he said, handing over a long envelope. "When we arrive in Baltimore, there will be plenty of hurly-burly on the street. You and I will have to go our separate ways from the depot to the hotel—we cannot be seen together again, or we might give our entire scheme away. But keep in mind, Nell, that I won't be far behind you in case trouble should arise."

I nodded solemnly and tucked the envelope into my black knit bag. Looking out at the city of Washington, tinged in a pinkish gold as the new day was dawning, I let out a deep sigh. Mr. Pinkerton gazed out, too, for a few moments more, then turned and extended his hand for me to shake.

"I have business to attend to," he began, his arm

pumping mine like he was trying to fill a water bucket. "But I presume you can find a way to entertain yourself for a few hours here in Washington before we catch our train. There are plenty of candy shops and bookstores for you to explore."

Or fashion emporiums, I wanted to add.

"Do you think you can handle this, Nell?"

He didn't have to ask me twice. I shook the bag at my elbow and heard the jangle of my coins. Finally a chance to explore a big city and spend a little of the hard-earned money I'd saved.

With my green-gloved hand in his brawny one, I gave Mr. Pinkerton a firm shake and assured him that, indeed, I could.

Hours later, when we returned to Baltimore, the streets were as busy and stirred up as a beehive. It couldn't have been more different from our nighttime passing, when the city was sleeping. Rowdy crowds were pushing this way and that, and a fire engine pulled by six straining horses went careening down the center of the street. The dust kicked up by so many boots and animals made me sneeze. Adding that to the noisy chaos and the shoving bodies, and suddenly I felt turned around.

Which way was the Barnum Hotel? And what if my charade as Matilda Maddox had already been figured out? What if an angry mob of secessionists was waiting to grab me—what would I do? What would *they* do?

I pushed my way north a block or so, trying to get away from the heated throng near the depot. I passed a hotel and glanced up at a black-iron balcony, where a bearded man was shouting hate-filled words to the hordes below on the street. A fistfight broke out between two boys, and a third began throwing rotten eggs into the crowd. I could hardly breathe for the dust and the thick cloud of danger that hung in the air.

When I rounded another corner, I took a moment to lean against a white storefront until I could catch my breath and calm my jittery nerves.

"Matilda Maddox, you look like you're up to something!" came a voice. "I'm so glad I can keep my eye on you again."

I whipped around, fearing the worst was about to unfold as I faced the secessionist acquaintances I'd made during our stay here. But to my great surprise and relief, I was gazing right into the face of Aunt Kate herself. I wanted to throw my arms around her and make sure I wasn't dreaming. But I knew my aunt was never one to make a fuss—especially not smack in the middle of a public street.

"What a relief to see you!" I said, grateful to have those fierce blue eyes before me again. I hastily scanned her face, her arms, her hands, just to comfort myself that she wasn't hurt or injured in some way. "Has it been hard for you today? Have there been any threats?"

"Threats, yes," she said, dropping her voice low and stepping closer. "But not against you and me. The threats are against Mr. Lincoln in the hopes of keeping him from the presidency. I fear that even after he puts his hand on the Bible and finally swears the oath of office, he still won't be safe. Some of these folks won't be satisfied until they put Mr. Lincoln in a grave."

A few menacing drunks pushed past, knocking both Aunt Kate and me off balance. I bumped into a man and his wife as they were passing on the other side of us and nearly fell to my knees. He grabbed my arms just in time and righted me.

"There you go, miss," he said, and immediately I recognized that deep, gravelly voice. It was Detective Webster. He and Hattie Lawton were arm in arm like a married couple, probably on their way to our meeting at the Barnum Hotel. "Don't let anyone knock you around, you hear?"

I smiled and thanked him for his help, mindful not to expose their true identities, and watched them walk on down the busy street and deeper into the angry mass. How I hoped they would be safe. A chill raced through me, and I pulled my coat tighter against the February cold.

"Look to your left," my aunt said softly, her voice close to my ear now as she pretended to dust off my wool wrap, "but don't make a show of it."

As casually as I could, I turned to my left and glanced around. Just across the busy street, slipping a coin to a newspaper boy, stood Mr. Pinkerton. He shot a quick nod to the two of us and ran his finger along the side of his nose as if giving a miniature salute. Then he moved on into the throng and disappeared in the same direction as Hattie Lawton and Detective Webster.

It was our turn to move along now. But I hesitated, unsure whether I had the courage to push through Baltimore's angry mobs, mindful of what might be waiting for us when we gathered at the Barnum Hotel.

Be fearless, Detective Webster had encouraged, *in everything you do. Fearless.*

"You seem a little taller to me today, Nell," Aunt Kate said softly, looping her arm through mine and setting us off. I was surprised she didn't stick with calling me Matilda, but maybe she was a little tired from her late night.

"Perhaps I am," I said, matching my steps to hers as we began our march together through the dangerous city. It was late afternoon now, and the sun was a vivid orange—nearly red—as it began to sink lower in the western sky.

Aunt Kate tilted her head to the side as we pressed on down the wooden-plank sidewalk, both of us making a *tip-tap* sound as we went.

"What's this, Nell? Maybe it's the pandemonium that comes and goes around us affecting my hearing.

But from what I can tell by the sound of it, your boots aren't making their usual heavy thumping."

And that's what you get by spending time with detectives. They don't miss a thing. And they're not shy about digging into your personal business for useful information.

"That's right, Aunt Kate. They're not."

And even though there was nothing but ruffians all about us, I couldn't help but glance side to side to make sure I wasn't going to offend anyone's sense of decency. Then I lifted the hem of my dress and my many layers of petticoats, and I stuck out my left foot.

Aunt Kate gasped and threw both her blue-gloved hands to her cheeks. She was marveling at what she saw—a brand-new pair of ladies' boots. And they were beauties: delicate white, narrowing to a point in the front. There was a row of tiny black buttons, which had taken an eternity to fasten back at the fashion emporium in Washington, running all the way up my ankle. And best of all was the wedged heel, about one inch high, which made me feel like I was eye to eye with Aunt Kate now.

"What about the old ones?" she inquired, shaking

her head in disbelief. "What about your father's old, brown boots?"

"I believe that old pair has served me well, Aunt," I said with a grin. And looping my arm right back into hers, I was the one who set us off down the sidewalk this time. While I didn't quite speed us up to her usual fast walking, I did push on with a firm, steady step. "But I thought it was about time to make a fresh start."

I could feel Aunt Kate peeking at me as we walked. And when I finally stole a glance in her direction, the smile I saw in her eyes let me know how much she approved.

"Care for a licorice?" she asked, slipping the familiar silver tin from her coat pocket and flicking it open.

"No, thank you," I replied. And as smoothly as I could, I offered her my own brand-new tin. "Would you like a butterscotch?"

Aunt Kate gave me a quizzical look as she reached over and popped a yellow candy in her mouth. A carriage raced past us, a few noisy rebels shouting whoops and rough words. But Aunt Kate and I ignored it as we pressed in close together, arms entwined, and set off again down the busy sidewalk and into the red-tinged twilight toward the Barnum Hotel.

It was just the two of us making our way through this great big mess of a city, but thoughts of so many others marched along with us in my mind—not only Cornelius but Matthew Warne. Jemma and brave Old Joseph Tuthill. Mama and my brothers. Detective Webster and Hattie Lawton. Mr. Pinkerton. And Mr. Bangs back in Chicago.

I might have given up my daddy's old boots, but I still carried a little piece of him—a piece of all of them—with me in my heart. Aunt Kate once said that family is the folks we choose to be with, not the ones we're stuck with. But I had my own notions about family now. To me, family meant taking the folks we're stuck with and choosing to love them anyway.

"Mind the puddle," Aunt Kate said as we hurried across the street ahead of another crowded carriage. I was paying attention to the noisy scene before us, but the words from Mr. Pinkerton's telegraph were echoing in my mind:

All right.

Everything was all right.

Even though there was evil afoot on this good green earth and angry cries at Mr. Lincoln from the Southerners. Even though the drumbeats of war were pounding from state to state. And even though the memory of that "Dixie"-whistling stranger still gave me chills, I knew I could face whatever may come.

Because I was not alone.

Because I was stronger than I'd ever dreamed.

And, most of all, because I had family to walk beside me.

Epilogue

In Which I Hear the Sweet Song of Liberty

March 4, 1861

Dear Jemma,

There is so much to catch you up on, I don't know that I can fit it all into one letter. First off, I saw the Maple Tree with my own eyes, and he is as hardy as ever. He misses you something awful, that's true, too. I fear the danger you'd put yourself in, but you'd surely be a help if you were working with him in the fight for freedom. I gave him your message, and do you know what he said? "That child's got gumption."

I am writing to you today from the steps of the Capitol building they are constructing here in Washington. It has been a few hours now since President Abraham Lincoln swore to "preserve, protect, and defend the United States Constitution." Most folks think he was jabbing at the South and those seven states that have broken away—secession is the right word, I think—from the rest of the Union. But what I hear in his words is the sweet song of liberty. I think what he is saying is that he's wanting to protect the rights of every one of us, slave and nonslave alike, to the pursuit of happiness.

I've been pursuing my own happiness this past week. I cannot share secrets—you know how the Pickled Onion is about information slipping into the wrong hands. But I will tell you that I arrived in

Washington safe and sound, along with a
special traveler. This individual was:

Lanky and a bit rumpled in appearance.
Intelligent.
New to Washington.
Clever.
Over six feet tall.
Likes butterscotch.
Nice to the ladies.

I have even more news for you, too,
as I seem to have landed myself a job.
Thank heavens for drunkards and fighters,
because their wicked ways have opened
the doors to my dreams.

I think you already know that I
am pretty fast with a pen. Well, a
correspondent for the *Amboy Times* broke
his hand in a bar fight around here a
few days back, so he asked me to do his
writing for him. He's been spending more and
more time back at the bar, so I guess he's
pretty comfortable with our arrangement.
I have already written a few newspaper

reports about President Lincoln's perilous journey through the dastardly city of Baltimore, where bloodthirsty thugs wanted to pierce his pure heart with a gleaming stiletto. And in a few hours, I'm going to telegraph my report on the spectacle of the inauguration—did you know Mr. Lincoln has grown a beard along his chin for this occasion, but no mustache?

The Pickled Onion says I'm a natural at telling stories. She says I could be editor of that newspaper by the time I am twenty. It is just like her to think a woman could take a man's job like that. But if the newspaper is full of drunks and bar brawlers like the one I've replaced, perhaps I can become an editor someday.

I'd say I have a good set of ears for this kind of work—spending time with the Pickled Onion sure has helped me in the arts of eavesdropping, spying, and general sneaking around. And I guess her drilling me in grammar and vocabulary has made me more ~~articulite expresive eloquant~~ good with words.

President Lincoln has said before that a house divided cannot stand. And I believe in my heart he's going to change things in this country soon. Can you imagine a United States where slavery is stamped out? I have been thinking a lot about all the promise that lies ahead.

I imagine a time when you will be able to move back from Canada and live free. And with all those things you're so good at—cooking and penmanship, your fast running and perfect aim, not to mention your own talent at listening in on what folks are gossiping about—we'll be able to piece your family back together. Even your uncle Ezekiel and the others. Just imagine the life you can stake out for yourself.

The Pickled Onion would sure love to know you.

I have to find a new name for her, since her face doesn't look nearly so sour these days and the bitterness is gone. We're no longer a house divided. And I have you and the Maple Tree to thank for that. You both helped me understand what happened back in Chemung County. Finally, we can lay that anger and sadness to rest.

I know lots of people are fearing the worst right now, as there is endless talk of a war between the states. But I cannot help but feel an ember of hope burning within me. Hope for you coming back from Canada, hope for me and the Pickled Onion getting along. And hope that Mr. Lincoln will not let our Union be ripped apart. I guess you could say I'm singing my own sweet song of liberty.

If young folks like us can't sing it, then who can?

Very truly your friend,
Nell

Author's Note

The Detective's Assistant is a work of fiction, and Nell Warne exists only in the pages of this book. But Kate Warne was a very real person. She and the characters of Allan Pinkerton, Timothy Webster, Hattie Lawton, George H. Bangs, and, of course, Abraham Lincoln were living, breathing contributors to America's history. Their lives and actions were the inspiration for this story.

The life of Kate Warne requires its own detective work to piece together. Her gravestone tells us she was born in Chemung County, New York. But little else can be found of her life before she entered Allan Pinkerton's

National Detective Agency office as a twenty-three-year-old widow. And while Pinkerton kept extensive files on his cases and his operatives, Chicago's Great Fire of 1871 destroyed most of his records.

When Kate Warne became the first female detective in the United States on August 23, 1856, Pinkerton was doing something almost unheard of: hiring a woman to do what was then seen as a man's job. Aside from mind-numbing factory work or running a boardinghouse, there were very few employment options for single or widowed women.

"I finally became convinced that it would be a good idea to employ her. True, it was the first experiment of the sort that had ever been tried; but we live in a progressive age, and in a progressive country. I therefore determined at least to try it, feeling that Mrs. Warne was a splendid subject with whom to begin," Pinkerton recalled in his book *The Expressman and the Detective* in 1874. "She succeeded far beyond my utmost expectations."

By one of the few accounts in her own words to survive, from *Herndon's Informants: Letters, Interviews, and Statements About Abraham Lincoln,* we see that Kate Warne had a determined personality and was no pushover. In order to protect Lincoln on his train ride through deadly Baltimore, it was crucial that Kate arrange sleeping compartments together at the back of the train. But this was not an easy task: "Any person could take a Berth where they pleased. I gave the Conductor half a dollar to keep my berths, and by standing right by myself we manage[d] to keep them."

The most we can learn about Kate Warne comes from Pinkerton's accounts of the many exciting cases he and his detectives solved. While the cases presented in this novel are works of fiction, they are inspired by her real exploits, which can be found in Pinkerton's books *The Somnambulist and the Detective: The Murderer and the Fortune Teller* (1875) and *The Spy of the Rebellion* (1883), along with *The Expressman and the Detective*.

"Kate Warne felt sure she was going to win," Pinkerton wrote in *The Expressman and the Detective* as they closed in on Mr. Maroney's stolen money. "She always felt so, and I never knew her to be beaten."

But Pinkerton's experiment with female detectives was relatively brief. And if a girl like Nell wanted to follow in Kate Warne's footsteps, she would have found those doors quickly slammed shut. Pinkerton's son Robert, who took over the business, disbanded the Female Detective Bureau in 1876, despite his father's angry protests. Women would not be hired for police or detective work again until the next century.

Pinkerton doesn't hold back praise for what he calls his two finest detectives, Kate Warne and Timothy Webster. "Mrs. Warne was the first lady whom I had ever employed," he writes in *The Somnambulist and the Detective*. "As a detective, she had no superior, and she was a lady of such refinement, tact, and discretion, that I never hesitated to entrust to her some of my most difficult undertakings."

Her undercover role as Mrs. Barley, in particular, was key to successfully thwarting the Baltimore Plot, which was the most important case of Pinkerton's long career. The coded telegraph that appears in the book upon Lincoln's safe arrival in Washington is an exact message that Pinkerton sent out heralding their triumph:

```
G. H. Bang's
8O. Washington Street.
Chicago.
Plums has Nuts-arri'd at
Barley-all right.
```

Begun in 1850 in Chicago, the Pinkerton National Detective Agency quickly gained national prominence for catching train robbers and solving bank heists. The Pinkerton name came to mean "private eye" or private investigator, and the company's logo of an unblinking eye above the phrase *We never sleep* was nationally recognized. Pinkerton has written that Kate Warne never slept a wink during the train ride delivering Lincoln through Baltimore, just as the logo promised. The hard work of Kate Warne and the other operatives in protecting Lincoln leading up to his March 4, 1861, inauguration eventually grew into what we know today as the Secret Service, which protects all US presidents.

Pinkerton served President Lincoln throughout most of the Civil War, both protecting him from personal harm as well as spying on the South. And his National Detective Agency went on to chase down outlaws over the ensuing decades, including Jesse James, the Reno Brothers, and Butch Cassidy. But Pinkerton, Kate Warne, and Timothy Webster were not serving President Lincoln in April 1865 when actor John Wilkes Booth fired the fatal shots in Lincoln's assassination.

By that time, Timothy Webster had already died.

At the outbreak of the Civil War, he'd gone under-cover as a Confederate soldier of the South. With Hat-tie Lawton portraying his wife, the bold pair delivered valuable information to the Northern army. But he was eventually found out and hanged as a spy in April 1862. He was forty years old. Hattie Lawton stayed with him until the end, served time in a Confederate prison, then was never heard from again.

Kate Warne continued her detective work during the Civil War, working with Pinkerton and posing as a Southern belle. A master of disguises and false identities, Kate Warne went by many aliases, such as Kay Warne, Kay Waren, and Kitty Warren. She was known to close friends simply as Kitty.

Vibrant and full of life, Kate Warne died in 1868—felled not by a murderer or sworn enemy, but by pneumonia. She was just thirty-five. With no other family to her name, Allan Pinkerton was there by her side.

To this day, you can honor the memories of Kate Warne, Allan Pinkerton, Timothy Webster, and George H. Bangs at Chicago's Graceland Cemetery. Their grave-stones can be found—all together—in the Pinkerton family plot.

Answers to Ciphers

Page 54: Maple Tree = Old Joseph Tuthill, Jemma's father

Page 85: "It is very possible the Pickled Onion is able to 18 5 1 4 / 20 8 5 / 19 20 1 18 19!"

The puzzle can be solved by writing down the alphabet, then assigning a corresponding number to each letter. A=1, B=2, C=3, and so on, all the way to Z=26.

The answer to this cipher is READ THE STARS!

Page 101: When spoken out loud, "Phil O'Dell for ya" sounds like "Philadelphia."

Page 128: Rearrange the letters in *lemony notes* to form the words *stolen money*. (The letters also spell *stoney melon*, but that's just a funny coincidence, not the reason Nell was in Philadelphia.)

Page 179: "The Pickled Onion seems to take a Colt

along with her now, but not the kind that needs a sad-dle." Nell is talking about Aunt Kitty's Colt revolver.

Page 195: "Well, we're down where Mrs. Ippy lives now, if you catch my meaning." When spoken out loud, "Mrs. Ippy" sounds like "Mississippi."

Page 214: "The Pickled Onion even gets to XBMYY ZK XZYLWZYMY!*"
   * X=D, Y=S, and Z=I
   Solve the puzzle by substituting a D wherever you see an X, an S wherever you see a Y, an I where you see a Z, and testing other letters until you decipher the code. Extra hint: M=E
   Answer = DRESS IN DISGUISES!

Page 237: "maerc deci allinav" = *vanilla iced cream,* written backward

Page 281: "He lives at the corner where two streets meet. One street is a number—the age your brother was when he died of scarlet fever. The other is some-thing I used to put in your hair to scare you."
   These are clues from when Jemma and Nell were

young girls together. Nell's brother died at age seventeen. And Jemma used to put grasshoppers, or locusts, in Nell's hair. So the house where Old Joseph works is at Seventeenth and Locust Streets.

Page 343: "But I will tell you that I arrived in Washington safe and sound, along with a special traveler. This individual was:

Lanky and a bit rumpled in appearance.

Intelligent.

New to Washington.

Clever.

Over six feet tall.

Likes butterscotch.

Nice to the ladies."

This spells out:

L

I

N

C

O

L

N

If You Want to Read More

I love looking at old photographs and poking around in ancient books. If you're as curious as I am about old stories, you might enjoy reading Allan Pinkerton's action-packed adventures featuring Kate Warne. Look for *The Expressman and the Detective* (W. B. Keen, Cooke, 1874), *The Somnambulist and the Detective: The Murderer and the Fortune Teller* (W. B. Keen, Cooke, 1875), and *The Spy of the Rebellion* (G. W. Carleton, 1883).

I also think it's fun to dig up old newspapers to see what daily life was like. Now that most newspapers are archived online, research has become easier. You can find great nuggets from history, such as the *Chicago Press & Tribune* description of the Pinkerton detectives threatening "genteel rascality" that ran on page 166. That account was published January 21, 1857, though I placed it a few years later in the book. I found the *Amboy Times* description of Abraham Lincoln as "crooked-legged" on July 24, 1856, to be hilarious (page 47). And I couldn't resist updating the plot with the *Chicago Press & Tribune* story from October 2, 1860, that included mention of a "fine Glee Club" (page 244).

There are many websites that feature full transcripts of Abraham Lincoln's speeches and writing. One of the most helpful sites I relied on was The Lincoln Log: A Daily Chronology of the Life of Abraham Lincoln. The site is part of the Papers of Abraham Lincoln, a project of the Illinois Historic Preservation Agency and the Abraham Lincoln Presidential Library and Museum. It can be found at thelincolnlog.org.

For Older Readers

If you want books that aren't more than a hundred years old, you can look through some recent nonfiction titles that examine this part of American history. Many are fast-paced accounts, not anything stuffy and boring. The best-researched books I enjoyed were Michael J. Kline's *The Baltimore Plot: The First Conspiracy to Assassinate Abraham Lincoln* (Westholme, 2008) and Daniel Stashower's *The Hour of Peril: The Secret Plot to Murder Lincoln Before the Civil War* (Minotaur Books, 2013).

Sometimes when you're writing, you have to figure out the little details before you can capture the bigger picture. And that can make for some amusing titles to check out from the library, such as C. Willet and Phillis Cunnington's *The History of Underclothes* (Michael Joseph, 1951) and Martha Vicinus's *Suffer and Be Still: Women in the Victorian Age* (Indiana University Press, 1972). I also relied on Wendy Gamber's *The Boardinghouse in Nineteenth-Century America* (Johns Hopkins University Press, 2007).

Acknowledgments

There is the solitary act of writing, and then there is the communal effort of bringing a story into the world. I am grateful to my writing group—Carol Fisher Saller, Linda Kimball, Elizabeth Fama, and Susan Fine—for their support and guidance through the years. Esther Hershenhorn has been an amazing booster and mentor. Irene Fahrenwald, librarian to the stars and an early reader of this story, gave me great insights. Angela Sherrill infected me with her crazy love of children's literature. Franny Billingsley generously shared writing advice. Jennifer Fleming listened to every up and down. Jennifer Mattson helped me through countless drafts and plot twists with her usual grace and calm. My husband, Norm Issa, patiently read every word. And, of course, there are Dad and Mom: Harry and Kathleen Hannigan have been unfailing champions of my writing life, starting with my earliest days penning homemade birthday cards. I thank you all.

Kate Hannigan does her own sort of detective work when she researches stories. A former newspaper journalist, she writes fiction and nonfiction books for young readers. She invites you to visit her online at katehannigan.com.